UNDERNEATH IT ALL

The UnBRCAble Women Series, #3

By

KATHRYN R. BIEL

KATHRYN R. BIEL

UNDERNEATH IT ALL, The UnBRCAble Women Series, #3

Copyright © 2020 by Kathryn R. Biel

Ebook ISBN-13: 978-1-949424-10-2
Paperback ISBN-13: 978-1-949424-11-9

Cover design by Becky Monson

DEDICATION

To all the default parents out there:
I see you. I hear you. I feel you.
You've got this.

CHAPTER 1

Perfect.

I turn this way and that, searching the reflection in the mirror for hidden flaws. Something that jumps out and screams, "This is all wrong!"

But I can't find anything.

This dress is perfect for me.

It doesn't hurt that I've had barely anything to eat all week besides grapefruit and black coffee. My head has been pounding as a result, but it doesn't matter. The sacrifice is worth it to look this good.

Also, I may be wearing two pairs of Spanx underneath the dress.

Large Marge my ass.

I want all the haters to see that you could bounce a quarter off that ass. It doesn't matter that those haters were from elementary school. It doesn't matter that I haven't been overweight since I was eleven. It doesn't matter that I can't breathe.

Mike walks into our large closet. Damn. I wanted to be totally put together and finished before he saw me. I like doing the big reveal, like something out of a movie. Since he picked this dress out for me, I wanted everything to be ... well, perfect ... when he first saw me in it.

And now it's ruined.

"Mike! I'm not ready yet. You can't see me until I'm finished." I try to push him out of our spacious closet.

He barely looks at me, which I must admit stings a bit. Am I disappointing in this dress? Did he think it would look better than it does? Why won't he stop and admire me like I so want him to?

Need him to.

"Relax, Marg. It's not *our* wedding. You look fine. Stop stressing about it. Frankly, I wish we could skip it all together. I barely know the bloke." Mike laughs a bit, mocking the groom's British accent and colloquialisms.

"But I know the bride. We're friends."

He's carefully combing through his extensive selection of ties, looking for just the right one. He glances back at my dress once, twice, three times.

It'd be easier to give him the hex code so he can match exactly. I think he'd prefer that.

It would make his precision so much quicker.

This is why we are so well suited to each other. I understand his need to have everything just so, and I've spent almost twenty years making it that way for him. He doesn't even have to ask most of the time; I know what he wants before he does.

I step closer, and he begins holding ties to my hip. He's narrowed it down to two.

"I think you should go with this one," I offer, pointing to the gray one with small red accents. The gray will look better with his black pinstripe suit and crisp white shirt.

Mike glances up at the ceiling. "The light's terrible in here. We need better light bulbs. No more of this LED crap. I want real light."

I make a mental note to try to find old-school incandescent light bulbs somewhere. I think I remember reading that they're illegal now, but someone's got to have them, right? It's critical to have proper lighting for color selection.

He puts a hand on my hip and pushes me out to the bedroom. He holds a blue and red paisley tie against my dress. It looks like something out of the wardrobe department from a 1980s teen flick, and Mike is cast as "yuppie male number one."

After an agonizing five minutes, he's settled on the gray tie, and I can go back to getting ready. I had my hair done this morning, nails and waxing done yesterday.

I've probably done more preparation than the bridal party.

That's the thing though. With each passing year, it takes longer and longer to look this put together.

Gone are the days when I could roll out of bed and look like a natural beauty.

Gone, also, are the days when I could wear a dress without scaffolding underneath it.

Pretty soon, makeup and Spanx won't be able to combat the toll my forty-five years on this Earth have taken on my body. Even I know more drastic measures lie in my future.

At least I've already got a great plastic surgeon.

I glance down at my ample cleavage, threatening to spill out of the plunging neckline of my dress. Dr. Chung did a great job with my implants.

God, I hate them.

As appearance focused as I know I can be, I'd never have had implants done if I didn't have to.

But I did.

Once you hear the news that you have a genetic mutation that has already caused you to develop breast cancer, the decision is pretty straightforward.

Not to mention Mike was all in favor of the reconstruction after my double mastectomy. I went larger than I'd been before. Nursing two babies had done a number on my boobs, and I'm sure I'd have been considering a lift at least, if the cancer hadn't intervened.

And if it weren't for my genetic predisposition to cancer, I wouldn't know anyone at this wedding. It'd be another one of those events that I endured for the sake of Mike and his *business* and his *career*. He makes good money in insurance and financial planning, but it's not like he's saving anyone's life or anything.

Though to listen to him talk shop, you might think otherwise.

This wedding will be so much better than one of his regular work events. One of his staff members, Sterling Kane, is marrying a woman I know from my UnBRCAble support group. Millie is one of the nicest people I've ever met, so I'm happy that she's getting her fairy tale and all.

It's what every girl wants, right?

Growing up in a family as dysfunctional as mine, I know it's what I always wanted. And I have it too. I used to lock myself in my room and dream of a life without bullying. Without taunting. Without screaming.

I used to dream of what I have right now.

The great husband. The beautiful house. Two kids, although they're teens, so you know how that goes.

Not to mention, it's been eons since Mike and I went out. We're long overdue for a romantic night. I used to laugh when people would talk about scheduling date night and sex like it was an appointment, but now I see how that might have been helpful as our lives got busier and busier.

Tonight, I've got plans. Mike must too, since he's the one who picked this dress out for me. I'll admit I was surprised, as he doesn't normally buy clothes for me, but there it was, in the trunk of his car.

I was even more surprised that he chose a fire-engine red for me, as he always told me blues and greens looked better with my blue eyes and honey-colored hair.

But I appreciated his vote of confidence that I was a size four, though truth be told, I'm more of a size six these days. Well, I was, but I was bound and determined to get into this little number for Millie's wedding. If I didn't do it before the holidays, there was no way this dress was fitting. So, grapefruit and black coffee it was.

I hope Mike appreciates it.

I do one last turn. Yes, it's perfect.

At least as close to perfect as I'm going to get tonight.

~~~***~~~

"Erin, this is my husband, Mike."

"Ah, yes. Mike. We've heard a lot about you in group." Erin extends a hand to my husband.

"All good, I hope," Mike laughs, uneasily.

"Of course, darling. What would I have to complain about? You're a stellar example of how a man should be," I gush. "You've been so supportive of me during my surgery and recovery, and you're so complimentary of my breasts. And this dress that you picked out is perfect for me." I smile at him.

How did I ever get so lucky?

And because my husband is not only kind and considerate but also humble, he blushes at my compliments. His gaze drops to his feet. I wish every person knew what it was like to be loved and cared for in this way. This truly is the fairy tale that we all dream of living.

At least the one I'd always dreamed of as a child.

I take his hand and give him a little squeeze. "Erin, congratulations on your engagement, again. I can't believe Xander proposed at Millie's wedding!"

Which, by the way, is totally a big no. You don't usurp someone else's day with your own thing. It's just not done.

"I know! I would be furious at him for doing this here, but apparently Millie put him up to it. It was actually *her* idea!"

I'm happy to hear Erin also has reservations about it. It's really not okay. I would have *flipped* if one of my bridesmaids did something like this to me. When Mike's sister got married, we'd found out we were expecting Bailey just that week. I hid my pregnancy, tossing my drinks in plants and "misplacing" them so no one was the wiser.

This day belongs to the bride and no one else.

Millie deserves to have a day that's all about her, especially after the long, hard journey she's had.

"Well, it's exciting nonetheless. Are you going to get married before the baby is born?" My gaze darts down to Erin's midsection. I try to remember how far along she is. Six—or is it seven—months? Reflexively, I find myself tightening up my stomach muscles, trying to make my tummy look flatter, as if the pregnancy belly is a contagious condition.

It would take a medical miracle for me to come down with a pregnancy.

Erin laughs. Her face is radiant and glowing. Xander sneaks up behind her and threads his arms around her belly.

"What's so funny?" he asks, planting a gentle kiss on her temple.

God, I miss being newly in love.

"Marg just asked if we're going to get married before the baby is born. I can't even process that you asked me to marry you, let alone a wedding. I haven't even started a Pinterest board for that!"

"Yes, well, better not to rush things then, right?" I chime in, not sure what else to say. Besides sitting next to Erin during a pedicure one time, and the occasional interaction during group, I don't know her all that well.

I mean, I know more than most acquaintances would because we share so much in group. But it's not like we're having sleepovers or meeting over coffee to solve the world's problems.

Not that I have many problems to solve. My cancer was small and caught incredibly early. My surgery, over five years ago now, went great. No complications. I've even completed my run with Tamoxifen, so I'm good to go. Mike loves the way I look. I had about the best surgical results you could ask for. Certainly nothing to complain about here.

I run my hands over my middle, sucking in again. It's then I realize that Mike has drifted off. Xander can't stop touching Erin, yet Mike is over at the bar.

Again.

I place my champagne flute on a nearby table. It looks like I'm going to be driving home tonight.

Might as well head to the powder room while he's getting another drink.

Once in the stall, it takes me a bit to wrangle the Spanx up and down. Frankly, I'm lucky I don't pee all over myself while trying to peel it off. I spend more time than I'd like to admit watching those videos that pop up on Instagram where the ladies just roll up the shapewear and—poof!—they're ten pounds lighter.

If only it worked like that in real life.

"And did you see her?"

I hear the voices as the door swings open. From the sound of it, there are at least three women.

"I can't believe it. I mean, who does that? At someone else's wedding, no less."

I want to burst out of the stall and defend poor Erin, but these ladies have a point. I don't care if Millie put Xander up to it. It's in poor taste.

Also, I'm hanging out of my Spanx with my dress up around my armpits. I'll just have to mentally defend Erin.

"I mean, what was she thinking? Could she be any more trashy?"

Okay, now that does it. Just because Erin's pregnant and only now getting engaged, it doesn't make her trashy. She doesn't have the time to wait! Don't these women know about BRCA? They should if they know Millie.

As soon as I can get my spandex back up, I'll charge out there and set these women straight.

"I don't think she could look any more pitiful, wearing that tiny skintight minidress."

Wait? Tight? Minidress?

That's certainly not what Erin's wearing.

"Nothing screams 'I'm a middle-aged Karen' than wearing a dress like that to a wedding. It'd be great for clubbing. On a twenty-year-old."

"But if you tell her that, she'll ask to speak to the manager."

The trio laughs. Finally, as the door opens, I hear one say, "If I ever wear a trashy red dress like that when I'm in my forties, please kill me. I'd die if I ever looked that desperate in public."

The door closes, leaving me alone again in the ladies' room.

In my skintight, red, desperate minidress.

I will not cry. I will not cry. I will not cry.

Squaring my shoulders, I march straight across the dance floor to the bar, where Mike is chatting it up with I don't even care who.

"I'd like to leave. I'm not feeling well."

Mike turns to look at me as if I have three heads. "But I just got my drink. And I'm having a good time."

I raise my eyebrow.

"Fine," he mutters, quickly downing the rest of his drink. "You know what they say, happy wife, happy life."

I don't dignify that jab with a response.

Mike doesn't either, and the ride home is filled with stony silence.

Great. What a perfect way to end the night.

CHAPTER 2

Desperate.

It's been three days, and the word is still coursing through my brain. It's quickly gaining ground with my other two trigger words: large and ho.

At least desperate doesn't rhyme with my name.

But it's left me virtually paralyzed. I can't get dressed. Suddenly everything in my closet, not to mention every beauty product on my vanity, seems desperate.

I text Becky again.

Don't lie to me.

She responds immediately.

I won't. You aren't desperate. You're hot and they're jealous that they'll never look that good, even in their prime.

Wait, is Becky saying I'm past my prime?

Hell, even I have to admit it—I am. I don't know exactly when I hit my prime, but it was long before the age of forty-five. It's not fair. Most men can still hit their prime.

But mine came and went, and I must have missed it. Did it happen while I was running around after toddlers or driving the kids to soccer practice? Was it the year I had the mastectomy and reconstruction? Surely it didn't happen while I was cleaning or planting flowers along the driveway.

I will be so pissed if I missed my prime because I was vacuuming.

I'm still ruminating about this when I pick Jordan up from swim practice. He pulls the back door of my Porsche Cayenne open and throws his backpack in. He carries virtually the entire contents of his locker in there, and it must weigh at least forty pounds. The last time I tried to lift it, I peed my pants.

My bladder is definitely past its prime.

He grunts in response to my greeting. I know better than to ask him how practice or his day went until he gets some food in him. The smell of chlorine fills my car. I glance at the clock on the dashboard. He was late getting out, again, which means I'm going to be late for my UnBRCAble meeting.

I hate being late.

Being late means you don't value someone else's time. I never want anyone to think I don't value them.

It's a terrible feeling.

I also hate that he doesn't greet me when he gets into the car. What must it look like to all the other parents whose kids greet them with a smile and gratitude?

I'd press the issue, but my head throbs, and my intestines are cramping again. I've spent most of the day in and out of the bathroom, which has not been pleasant. However, if it keeps me from gaining weight, I will deal with it. I'm too tired and drained to get into another fight with him.

"Dinner's waiting for you. Please remind Bailey to eat. I'll be home after my meeting," I call as Jordan slides out of the passenger seat. "Don't forget to do your homework."

"I did it before practice," he says finally. "Did you already eat?"

I nod, though I didn't. "Bailey didn't, so make sure she gets hers before you eat it all. Oh, and leave a plate for Dad."

Jordan tilts his head. "He's not home tonight either?"

Either.

Guilt floods me, and I'm tempted to pull into the garage and stay home with my son. But I didn't cancel ahead for UnBRCAble, so how would that look if I simply didn't show up?

"Dad had to work late. You know his job is demanding. His co-worker is on his honeymoon, so Dad has to pick up the slack. I don't know what they'd do without him."

But my sixteen-year-old has moved on, slamming the door and tromping off into the house to strap on the feed bag. I don't blame him. He burns thousands of calories during practice, not to mention his teenage metabolism that's currently in overdrive.

I may have to go back to work full-time, if only to cover the food bills while he's in high school.

Bailey's in eighth grade, so it wouldn't be too terrible if I did work more hours. It's not like the ten hours a week I spend doing bookkeeping from home is that taxing. I've certainly taken the time I needed to be there for the kids. Room mother, PTO board member (several terms), chair of the booster club for athletics at the junior high. I've made costumes and props for school plays and provided for more bake sales than I can even count.

Being a good mother is a full-time job.

Once we get through the holidays, which are rapidly approaching, I'll talk to Mike about it. See what he thinks.

I don't want to do anything that makes my kids' lives harder or more difficult, and working more hours might come at a cost to Jordan and Bailey.

As I pull into the parking lot at the Genevieve T. Wunderlich Women's Health Center where my UnBRCAble meeting is held, I sit for a minute. I'm beat, and if I weren't on the verge of being late, I'd consider closing my eyes. I was up late for Millie's wedding on Saturday, and it's as if I've been playing catch up ever since. I mean, who gets married the first weekend in December? It's such a busy time already, and I can't be out gallivanting until midnight without repercussions.

I am past my prime.

I shoot a quick text to Becky, inquiring how she made out with her parent-teacher conference. Her kids are great, but her youngest struggles with reading, so these conferences are always stressful on her. I wish she could see that Jackson will be fine because he's got the world's best mother.

Now, I need to get out of my car and get inside before I really am late. I wonder how much discussion there will be in the group tonight about Millie's wedding. Erin and Claudia were bridesmaids. I was the only other person from this support group there, and that was only because Mike works with Sterling. It would be insensitive and inappropriate to discuss in a room full of people who were not invited.

I know what it's like to be left out, and I would never want anyone else to feel that pain.

On the other hand, Erin did get engaged at Millie's wedding. Even five days later, I still have a problem with it. Not as big of a problem as I have with those three girls in the bathroom though.

All in all, I'm not in a great place, so I really need some support this week. That's the thing about the UnBRCAble women—we don't have to be struggling related to our genetic mutations to receive encouragement and guidance. We may be here because of our genetics, but we're here for each other for all the other aspects of life too.

I push through the door, trying to compose myself on the way in. Just because I feel like a frazzled mess is no reason to look like one. I smooth my hair and brush it behind my shoulders.

Deep breath. I'm among friends. I will sit here and absorb the positive energy. I don't even have to tell them about what happened at the wedding. I will simply feel better by being in the—

What the hell?

The first thing I see is the shirt. It's the ugliest thing I've ever seen. I mean, how can one not see it?

It's orange. Bright, hurt your eyes orange. If that wasn't bad enough, there are neon green shapes at the bottom with white stick figures dancing in them. And who wears a Hawaiian shirt in December?

As bad as the shirt is, that's not the worst part.

The worst part is who is wearing it.

A man.

A man sitting all relaxed and cozy like he belongs here. Here in the group.

My group.

My group for women who have had mastectomies and hysterectomies and suffer from vaginal dryness and dying nipples.

Why is there a man in my nipple group?

Instead of screaming, because that isn't the polite thing to do, I calmly sit on the edge of an overstuffed loveseat and say, "What's *he* doing here?"

Okay, probably not as polite as I meant to be, but no. Just no. I cannot deal with this right now. The pounding in my head ramps up to the point where there's a decent chance it might actually explode.

Claudia looks over at me, her face trained and serene. Out of the corner of my eye, I'm sure I see Erin roll hers. "Hi, Marg. As you can see, we have a new member today. Why don't we all go around and introduce ourselves?"

I'm not sure if Claudia uses essential oils or smokes weed or what to always be so chill, but whatever she's using, I may need to get some. When it's my turn, I take a deep breath and will my face to have its neutral, pleasant look. "I'm Marg. That's with a hard g at the end. I'm BRCA-1, five years post-op. Had a great—" I start to say reconstruction, but how can I talk about breasts here with a man who is not my husband? "I'm fine now," I lamely finish.

As the next person is about to start, Millie comes through the door like a whirling dervish. "Sorry I'm late, everyone. Oh hey, this is new." She leans over and shakes the interloper's hand. "I'm Millie. BRCA-1. I'm a teacher, and I just got married!" She waves her hand, the diamonds glinting off the bands. Millie plops down onto a chair and smiles at the man as if he is one of us.

"Um, okay," he begins, his voice somewhat lower in register than I would have expected with that shirt. He is sucking on a lollipop like a two-year-old. He pulls the stick out of his mouth. "I'm Thom. That's Thom with an h." He looks at me when he says this. I know he's mocking me. I think I hate him already. "I did one of those genetic tests and found out I'm BRCA-2 positive, and I don't really know what that means, so I'm here to find out. Oh, and I should mention that I'm on the radio, so you may hear me talking about my journey there."

Millie claps her hands like an excited child. God, does she have to wear every emotion on her sleeve? "A star is in our midst! How exciting! What station?"

Thom smiles. "I'll leave that for you all to figure out. And congratulations on your marriage."

Then it hits me. Millie's here.

She's not on her honeymoon.

So why would Mike tell me he had to work late to cover for Sterling?

Our marriage is based on honesty and truth. Why is he lying to me?

CHAPTER 3

Today has got to be better.

I don't feel any better, but I checked the calendar on my phone, and it doesn't show anything besides the usual obligations, shuttling the kids around. I have Yoga Burn at ten, so I can get in a quick ride on my Peloton as soon as I drop the kids at school.

Maybe later I can squeeze in a nap and finally get rid of the bags under my eyes. I've been resorting to using cold spoons before I leave the house.

I put on my Fabletics leggings and carefully brush my hair into a low ponytail. Since going into surgically induced menopause at the age of thirty-nine, my hair has been one of the casualties. It's much finer than it ever was, and it breaks if I look at it too hard. Pulling it back is terrible on it, especially around my forehead.

There's a part of me that understands the need for the mom-bob, but I won't be one of *those* women who gives up on herself. I've worked too hard for too long to give up.

The morning is typically chaotic, with two barely awake teens and a way too early school start time. By quarter 'til seven, we're heading to the car, Bailey insisting she should get to ride in the front seat while Jordan shoves her out of the way.

"Guys, seriously, stop. You cannot be carrying on like a bunch of heathens. You'll wake the neighbors," I snap. We go through this at least twice a week.

And every time, it makes me wonder why I don't have them take the school bus.

Large Marge is in charge.

I shake my head, the voices from so long ago ringing in my ears as if they were in the same room. No, nothing good comes about from riding the bus. I can deal with my children's squabbling to spare them years of pain and anguish.

I want my children to know how much I love them, that I would do anything for them. Even if it means getting dressed and out of the house on days when I'd rather sleep in.

Once back in the house, I make my breakfast smoothie. Kale, blueberries, banana, orange juice, chia seeds, and kefir. While I'm sipping, I pick up the debris my family has strewn about. Some days—most days—it's hard to tell if a bomb went off or if my kids walked through.

Mike is no better. His overcoat from yesterday is thrown over the back of the dining room chair. He has to pass right by the coat hooks on the way to the kitchen. I will never understand why he can't hang it up when he walks in and through the mudroom. As I hang up his coat, my phone rings. Becky usually calls me on her way to work. I pull the phone from my leg pocket, dropping Mike's coat as I do.

"Why?" I say, not even bothering with a greeting. This is how Becky and I roll. We are both so busy with everything that most people would never be able to follow our conversations.

"Why what?" She doesn't miss a beat.

"Why," I say, bending over, "can my husband *not* hang his coat up? I trained the kids from the age of two, yet he is almost fifty and can't figure it out." As I shake the coat out, something flutters to the floor.

Great. Another thing for me to pick up.

I make my task into a squat, because at my age, you can never squat enough to keep the booty lifted.

Mid-squat, my heart stops as I see the print on the card.

"What's wrong?" Becky asks. Apparently I'm making some weird, strangled noise from the back of my throat.

I tell her what just happened. "You will never guess what it says."

"You know I won't, so just tell me. I'm almost to work."

"It's for Home Again Realty."

"Oh my God."

"I know." My pulse races, and I feel like my heart is going to jump out of my chest.

There's a silence on the line.

"Beck? You still there?"

"Do you want me to come over?"

Huh? "No, why? You have work." I don't want to keep her or make her late.

"Well, the card ... do you want some support?"

Support? "Why? You know what this means, right?" I can't even believe this is happening.

Another measured breath. "I think I do."

"He said he had to work late yesterday because he was working on my Christmas present. He did it. He's buying me that lake house we've been looking at out at Muskcoogan Lake!"

"You think?"

"What else could it be?" I start to jump up and down. We've talked about getting a place out there for years, but with the kids' hectic schedules, it never seemed like the right time. Now, we only have five years until we're empty nesters. "I don't know how I'm going to not let him know that I know. How many days until Christmas?"

We disconnect, my mind a flurry of what to do next. This changes everything.

I need to start shopping. I can probably wait until the after-holiday sales for most of the furnishings. I pull up the listing again on my phone, looking at the pictures. I'll certainly have my work cut out for me in the new year, but I know I can make this place perfect in time for Memorial Day. I can already see in my head the party we'll have out there to kick off summer.

Quickly, I find a site that does personalized home goods to order a sign that says, "Lake Life, Kensington Palace." A running joke based on our noble-sounding last name. I bookmark a few that I like. This news has my mind spinning so fast that I can't make a decision about which one is the perfect sign. I'll just have to make sure I open Mike's present before he opens mine on Christmas morning.

I wonder how he'll package this gift. Will he wrap up the keys to the front door? Or maybe a picture of the house? Oh, I know! I bet he wraps up the deed to the property in a fancy box.

I'm so busy with planning for our lake house that I skip the bike all together and even consider bailing Yoga Burn. But I make myself go. It's the holiday season after all, and I've never been able to resist Christmas cookies or a peppermint mocha from Starbucks. Now that I don't have to pour myself into that little red dress, I plan on indulging for the next three weeks.

When I walk into the studio, the instructor, Lia, gives me a puzzled look. "I thought you weren't going to be here today."

"I always come to the Thursday class. Why wouldn't I be here?"

She shrugs. "I thought you said something about a doctor's appointment or something."

Oh crap.

"I forgot all about it! They called to move it, and I didn't put it in my phone. If it's not in my phone, it doesn't exist!" I start to run out the door but stop. "I'm so sorry, Lia. Thank you for the reminder. Have a great day and I'll see you next Thursday."

No matter how rushed you are, there is no excuse for poor manners.

I practically fly across town and pray that Dr. Chung will still see me. The memory, which has been spotty more than I'd care to admit, comes back about having to reschedule my checkup to today. Of course, due to my flightiness, I'm not dressed appropriately for the doctor. Leggings, sports bra, and a tank top underneath my wool peacoat. Not to mention I didn't put makeup on, and my nails need to be filled. I look ridiculous. I can only hope the waiting room is empty.

But it's jam-packed. No one looks up, at least not that I can see. It's not as if most people want others to know they are visiting a plastic surgeon. I can hold my head high. I hadn't come here to improve an imperfection. I had visited this office to save my life.

It's been a few years since I've been in. I thought it was odd that they called for an appointment, but perhaps it's routine. Despite the fact that I've waited more than an hour to see the doctor during previous appointments, the office has a strict policy against tardiness. A full fifteen minutes late, I expect them to make me reschedule yet again.

"Yes, Ms. Kensington, so glad you made it. Follow me," the nurse instructs. I glance over my shoulder at the waiting room full of people. They were all definitely here before me. Well, I guess Dr. Chung knows I'll be quick in and out because everything seems good.

I mean, I probably should mention that my left side feels a little tight in the armpit. I noticed it after last week's Yoga Burn, and the nagging tug has hung out all week. Dr. Chung doesn't care about my middle-aged aches and pains though. He did a beautiful reconstruction, and that's all that matters.

The nurse takes my blood pressure and reviews my medications before excusing herself. As she's about to leave, I realize she forgot to give me a gown.

"Um, may I please have a gown to change into?"

Her gaze shifts to the tablet in her hands and then down to the ground. She doesn't look at me when she says, "I don't think you need to change today," before scurrying out. She must be new. She certainly has a lot to learn about bedside manner.

Thank goodness I'm only here for a quick well-check and don't have anything seriously going on.

CHAPTER 4

I stare at my computer, willing my eyes to process a different message than the screen is presenting. I squint, rub my eyes, close them, and open again.

Nope, it's still there.

By the way, when you receive devastating medical news, Google is the last place you should visit. However, I can firmly recommend visiting a bar. I'm kicking myself for not having a drink—or ten—but I still have to pick the kids up after school.

Recalled.

I've never thought much about that word. When it applied to my car, I simply took it in and had the airbags replaced. When it applied to lettuce, I simply threw it out. Now it applies to something purposefully placed in my body. You want to know the irony of it all? I got these implants to prevent getting cancer.

Thanks to some idiot at some company, my textured breast implants can cause me a different type of cancer.

As Dr. Chung explained this, I felt like I was having an out-of-body experience. It was worse than hearing about my cancer, since I already knew it was there, and even the original BRCA-mutation news. That was a little more of a shock since there wasn't a family history. But this? The timing on this could not be any worse. It's the second week in December. Doesn't Dr. Chung know how much I have to do?

But my motivation for it all—the shopping and baking and sending out cards and attending parties—has vanished. Even the excitement about the lake house seems like a distant memory.

All I can think about is having these silicone balls of death removed from my chest.

I stand up from my computer and pace. I need to call Mike, but I don't know how to say this over the phone. He's not going to be pleased. I can see him wanting to pursue a lawsuit against the manufacturers. More so, I can see him being upset that I'll be out of commission and recovering again.

This could not come at a worse possible time.

I need to talk to someone about this and reach for the phone to call Becky. My hand freezes before I can dial her. While she's been supportive, this is not something she understands. She doesn't get it. She was certainly supportive enough the first time, but she didn't *understand*.

She'll want to fix it for me, and she can't. I can't burden her with this. This is my load to carry.

And the thought of going through the pain again stops me cold. I'll have to. It's not like I have a choice.

I scroll through my phone to call Claudia from UnBRCAble instead. She will know the right things to say and talk me down.

Except her phone goes to voicemail. I leave a quick message about accidentally dialing her and not wanting her to think something was wrong. After all, I hate when people call out of the blue but don't leave a message.

I look through my phone again. I don't have anyone else's number. I could certainly reach out on Facebook or Instagram, but that seems impersonal.

Breathe, Margot Mary. You can do this.

You know things are serious when you talk to yourself and use your full name. But I'm right.

I don't need anyone to get me through this. I've got myself. How would it look if this *minor* setback threw me into a tailspin? I can't let anyone know I've spent the past three hours sobbing and hugging my knees.

Well, trying to hug my knees because my left armpit is sore.

I wash my face in cold water, brush my hair, and put on decent clothes. I consult the calendar. So much for looking to increase my work hours after the holidays.

It's December twelfth. My shopping is nowhere near done, and I haven't wrapped a single thing. The Christmas cards sit in the box they were shipped in. At least I had the forethought to order those two weeks ago.

The only thing in my favor is that the house is decorated.

That, and I'm a master list maker.

Twenty minutes later, I have a day-by-day list of what needs to get done. Once the list is cross-referenced with my calendar, it becomes clear.

I don't have time for this surgery.

Not with the holidays. Not with Jordan's double swim practices and Bailey's gymnastic classes over break. Not with tax season.

But I also can't live with the chance of developing lymphoma either.

Dr. Chung is usually scheduled out months for elective procedures, but he considers mine emergent.

That does not instill calmness or any reassurance.

A quick glance at the clock tells me I'm late getting dinner started. I've got to get everything prepped before I pick Bailey up at school and take her to the gym. Then it's home to start cooking before I race to pick up Jordan and then back to get Bailey.

It's hectic, but Thursdays are one of the few nights we get to eat together as a family during swim season. It's important for us to stay connected that way.

Plus, it'll give me a chance to tell Mike I have to have another surgery.

~~~**~~~

"What do you mean you have to have another reconstruction? They are fine," Mike grumbles, not looking at me as he shovels a forkful of food into his mouth. "That's going to be a pain. Your mother is *not* staying here this time. I cannot deal with that woman for another month. You can go stay with her."

Both kids are on their phones, not paying an ounce of attention to us.

My hand stills, midway to my mouth, the lettuce dangling off the fork precariously. Much like my grip on reality. "Excuse me? Did you just say that if I can't take care of myself while I'm recovering from major surgery, I can't stay here?"

Dr. Chung already told me this surgery wouldn't be nearly as bad. He'll make an incision, slip the implants out and pop the new ones in. Easy peasy lemon squeezy. Some soreness because the implants are under the muscle, but not terrible. Not that I'm going to tell Mike that. Not right now at least.

Mike looks up from his plate. "You know that's not what I meant. You are so sensitive sometimes. It'll be fine. I'm sure you can make it work; you always do."

Yes, I do. And if I were Samuel L. Jackson, I'd punctuate that statement with some colorful language.

"It's not as if I have a choice with this," I say through gritted teeth, my head throbbing with the tension. "They cause cancer. I have them in the first place so I don't *die* of cancer, and now this type causes it."

"Can we sue?" Of course, that's where Mike's mind goes.

"I don't know."

"When is this going to happen?"

"I don't know."

"Are you sure you need to have it done?" He keeps firing questions at me like a prosecuting attorney.

"I don't know." I'd read some conflicting stuff on the internet today. Maybe I don't technically *need* to have it done this instant, but there is no way I can sleep at night knowing I *could* develop cancer because of them. I hate the idea of knowing that there are these foreign bodies inside me, trying to plot my death.

It's bad enough that my genetics have already tried that.

"You really need to get some answers, Marg. I'd think you'd do your research before worrying your children like this."

I glance at my kids, who are still scrolling through their phones, oblivious to what I've said. Frankly, they don't even know I had cancer in the first place. I never wanted to worry them, and other than UnBRCAble, it's not like I'm one of those pink-ribbon-waving kind of people. It's private, and I like to keep it that way.

"Yes, I can see how trying this is on them." Typical teens, self-absorbed. Truth be told, I'm not sure they'd even notice I was incapacitated. I mean, they *probably* would if I didn't pick them up on time.

Probably.

I try to reassure Mike. "I'll get more answers soon. I'll put it to the group as well and see if anyone's sued, but I don't think I remember hearing about it before this. Regardless, I'm going to be laid up for a while. Maybe you can take some time off work?"

Mike spears another forkful of asparagus. "You know I've got that conference coming up. I've got to travel for it. Try to work around that."

I glance at the massive dry erase calendar hanging on the wall. "It's on the calendar. Though I still don't understand who holds a conference the week between Christmas and New Year's. Seems like it would be a bad time."

Mike carefully sets his fork down. "Well, this surgery is coming at a bad time. You don't hear me complaining, do you?"

I can feel us heading down the path of an argument, and I don't want the kids to see us fight. It's not good for them to grow up with their parents yelling at each other. I swore my kids would not grow up like I did, in a broken home with parents who hated each other. I am going to give them the perfect life.

I smile tightly. "I'll figure it out."

CHAPTER 5

I tap my manicured nails anxiously on the steering wheel. I've waited all week for my UnBRCAble meeting. I need to talk to the ladies about options for me. My head has been throbbing all day. I can't tell if it's too much caffeine or not enough. I should probably look into that.

I'm the first one in the door, which gives me the chance to sit in my favorite seat. I don't like sitting on the couches where you are practically on top of someone else. I need my space.

The usual members file in, and Claudia has barely called the group to order when I blurt out, "I'm sorry, but I really need to talk. I found out that there is a recall on my implants."

"You've got the textured ones? Bummer," Frances offers.

Bummer indeed.

"Yes, and I have to decide what to do. They say you don't need them out necessarily, but I don't want to leave them in. I—" I stop abruptly when the door opens and in walks Thom, lollipop stick in his mouth, clad in another hideous Hawaiian shirt.

Dear God, it's so ugly, it's practically offensive.

It's not one Hawaiian shirt—it's four different prints together. One on each arm and two different ones making up the front panels. It is so wrong it should be outlawed. My mouth hangs open as I stare.

And wait, the collar is another print, while the pocket is a sixth—sixth!—print. Reds, browns, aqua blues, yellows, and black assault my eyes as I try to comprehend what I'm seeing.

"That shirt," I say.

Thom spins around. "Isn't it great! It's like the melting pot of fabric."

"It's—"

"It's very bright," Millie cuts me off. She doesn't know me well, but I'm guessing what I was about to say was written all over my face.

Thom plops down directly opposite me and pulls the pop out of his mouth. "I didn't mean to interrupt. Were you saying something when I walked in?"

"No," I say quickly. I can't talk about this in front of him.

"Huh, cause as I walked in, I could have sworn you were talking."

"It doesn't matter." His shirt is hurting my eyes.

"Marg, are you concerned about getting your implants removed?" Claudia asks gently.

I suck in a quick breath. How am I supposed to talk about this with *him* here? It's as if my safe zone has up and disappeared. I wish I could melt into the chair and disappear. I thought I'd left this feeling behind when I graduated high school, but here it is again.

I look at my hands. "Yes. I can't keep these in obviously, but what happens if the next ones are recalled too? Or they leak? Or they have problems and I become deformed?"

You only have to sit through a meeting or two to realize what could go wrong here. I was so lucky to have my surgery go so well the first time.

"What kind of problems?" Thom asks.

"P ... problems," I stutter. It's not like I'm going to talk about nipple death with him.

Claudia gently eases in. "The skin, without any underlying breast tissue, is very thin and doesn't have a good blood supply. It can die very easily, especially the nipples. Many of us have had to have our nipples removed. Marg, you had a nipple-sparing procedure, right? You've still got your nipples?"

I feel the blood rushing to my face as I cross my arms over my chest. I will not let myself be bullied into feeling ashamed again. "And that's why this group is for women. So we can talk about these things and support each other in a safe manner."

There.

I said it.

"Excuse me?" Thom asks. "What are you saying?"

"I'm saying that I don't feel comfortable talking about these things with you here." I double down. "This is a group for women. You're a man. You don't belong here. You can't possibly understand. Plus, it's nearly Christmas, and you're wearing a Hawaiian shirt."

Okay, so the second part is actually irrelevant, but it's bugging me, so I feel it needs to be said. He does not follow the rules of social decorum.

He stands up. I will not let him intimidate me. I stand too. I'm wearing flat boots, and even so, Thom is only an inch or so taller than me. Good. Easier for me to stare him down. His gaze darts down and then back up to meet my own.

"Are you saying I don't belong here?"

"Yes." I maintain my stance, arms folded and back straight.

"Because I don't have nipples?"

"Y ..." I open and close my mouth, suddenly at a loss for what to say.

He continues, "Because I don't have an increased risk for cancer because of my BRCA-2 positive gene mutation?"

Now I clench my jaw.

"Because I can't also have a mastectomy to prevent breast cancer?"

I wrinkle my nose at him.

Claudia stands up. "Marg, why don't you have a seat?" She places her hand gently on my arm and steers me back to my chair. "I know change can be difficult, but Thom is going through a lot as well. We all have our place in this group. We are all UnBRCAble together."

~~~***~~~

Another Thursday morning, and I'm back at Dr. Chung's. I'm still seething about UnBRCAble yesterday. I mean, I *get* that Thom's going through the same things, sort of, but he's not really now, is he?

He's never going to have hot flashes or early menopause.

He's not going to find himself back at the plastic surgeon to discuss options because his implants are recalled.

I head into my appointment, first of the day, ready to get this over with. I want Dr. Chung to pop these puppies out, slide new ones in, and let's be done with it. I don't have time to consider anything else.

I mean, in a perfect world, I'd probably opt for a DIEP flap procedure. That's where they basically give me a tummy tuck and use the skin and fat from my abdomen to create new breasts. It would be a win-win all around, and maybe I'd finally be able to wear a dress without scaffolding underneath to smooth out my belly.

But that's a major procedure with major downtime, so it's off the table for me.

Like I said, in a perfect world. I only pretend my life is perfect.

This week I'm undressed, and Dr. Chung is doing his presurgical examination. Surgery is tentatively scheduled for the day after Christmas, which is seven short days from now.

Mike's going to have to cancel his conference. He's not thrilled about it, but what else can we do? It was having him cancel or having my mom stay with us while I recover.

He canceled.

"Hmm."

I don't like the sound of that. "What's 'hmm'? Is that a technical term?" I ask the doctor who is poking and prodding away.

He pulls the gown wide open and steps back, squinting a bit. "That left side is definitely higher."

I glance down. "Yeah, I've noticed it too." I shrug. "The muscles on my left are tighter than on the right. It's where I hold my stress."

Now he moves around and lifts my left arm up. He's pressing his two fingers into the side of my implant. For an area that doesn't have much sensation, this kind of hurts.

He doesn't say anything as he pokes and prods. Finally he steps back and peers down the end of his nose at me. "I think you may have a capsular contracture forming on the left. Any pain?"

I shake my head. "Not really. Just a little tight, but I pulled a muscle at Yoga Burn. Other than that, I feel great."

That's a lie. I feel like crap most of the time.

Okay, so my breasts feel great.

Truth be told, that's a lie too, because I can't really feel them at all.

"Yup, I feel great. Never felt better."

"Okay, well, then the procedure should be quick. Maybe an hour or so. You're getting your blood work today, correct? Assuming that comes back fine, I'll see you next Thursday."

And with that, Dr. Chung is gone.

I get dressed, relieved to have one more thing out of the way. I've got to finish up Christmas shopping and wrapping today. I'd rather go home, take a bottle of aspirin, and sleep for three days. I am exhausted, and this headache won't let up.

Sometimes, I hate the holidays. There's so much stress, who can enjoy them?

I check the lists on my phone and my calendar. No Yoga Burn for me again this week. I should probably cancel my membership until after the new year, even though I need the class now more than ever. This sucks, and I probably won't eat lunch since I won't be able to work those calories off.

Sometimes, I feel like I've been conscious of my weight for most of my life.

Probably because I have.

You don't get a nickname like Large Marge and not develop a complex. I always thought that if I was thin enough and pretty enough and perfect enough, the other kids wouldn't pick on me.

You know what? It seems to have worked. Everybody likes me now.

On the way home from the doctor's appointment, I turn on the radio, hoping I didn't miss my favorite radio segment of the week. It's the Morning Meltdown with TJ the DJ and Todd. Every Thursday, they do the "Jerk-Face Award," where listeners call or email in with a situation and then everyone chimes in with whether the caller was the jerk or if they were the victim of jerk-dom. I cannot believe the audacity of people sometimes. It's like they have no idea of common decency and manners and decorum.

Todd starts. "This week, we're not talking to a listener. Our own TJ the DJ believes he was the victim of a jerk-face last night, and he wants your opinion."

Oh boy, this should be good. Whenever TJ the DJ or Todd is the victim, the person they are talking about usually gets skewered and with good reason.

"So you all know that I've been on a health journey recently, which included a thorough screening. Well, as luck would have it, I tested positive for a genetic thing. While this genetic mutation—"

"So can we call you a mutant man?" Todd interjects.

"Totally. But this mutation can happen in both men and women, but women get sick from it more than men. Men get sick too though."

"Like how sick?"

"Like cancer sick and death. But I don't want you to worry. Now that I know, I can be proactive about things and not be blindsided."

"That's good, man," Todd assuages. "If for nothing else, that's why routine health screenings are important."

"Right, man. Plus, I know my family history, which ain't good, and I want to be on top of that."

I cringe at TJ the DJ's use of the word *ain't*. Since when did that become socially acceptable?

TJ the DJ continues. "So part of my being proactive is to find a support group to learn as much as I can. You know, I want to stay alive and all. Last night was my second time going. Once again, I'm the only dude there."

"Score. Any eligible picks to become the next future ex-Mrs. TJ the DJ?"

TJ the DJ laughs. "Couldn't even get that far. One woman had an issue with me being there. She told me I didn't deserve to be there because it's a group for people with nipples."

I slam on the brakes. Luckily, there's no one right behind me.

What did I just hear?

"Um, TJ, man, last time I checked, you have nipples."

"Right? She also insulted my shirt, telling me I can't wear my trademark Hawaiian shirts because it's winter. Let's put it out to the listeners. Call in and tell me, am I the a-hole for joining this group for a medical condition, which I possess, just because it's historically been female members? Do they have a right to ask me to leave? Who is the jerk-face in this situation?"

My mouth goes dry. I drive home as the radio station plays a song. I'm in my own garage before they come back on the air. Good thing, as I don't know if I could—or should—be driving while listening to this.

"How stupid is this woman to think men don't have nipples? She's obviously a loser."

"You should sue her."

"She sounds like a nasty B."

"No, man, TJ. You're not the a-hole. She is."

"Your shirts are awesome, man."

"She's definitely an uptight biotch."

"She's the jerk-face, no questions asked."

Then I hear *his* voice again. "Well, the public has spoken and it's clear. TJ the DJ is not in the wrong."

And suddenly, I'm back in middle school again, the furthest thing from popular and well liked.

No, I cannot let it go down like this. I no longer cower on the bus seat while people talk smack about me. I pull out my phone and hastily dial.

And redial.

And redial again.

With each beep of the busy signal, I grow more and more angry. This isn't supposed to be happening. I'm a good person. I take good care of my husband and kids and I volunteer. All I want is a safe space to talk about my female bits—or lack thereof—with people who understand and don't judge what I'm going through.

Finally, they move on and there's nothing left to do. I can't defend myself. I've been dubbed a Jerk-Face.

I wonder if there's a trophy for that.

CHAPTER 6

"But ..." My brain is a fog of anesthesia and sleep. My mouth is dry, and I feel as if I'm made of lead. "Wait, what?"

Dr. Chung looks me straight in the eye. "I could not put the new implants in. There was an extensive capsular contracture on the left and some forming on the right. Additionally, there appeared to be a low-grade infection on the left. We need to make sure it's all cleared up before we put anything else in there."

I glance down, but my chest is wrapped tightly with ace bandages. There are drain tubes again.

Yippee.

"I thought this was supposed to be easy," I say, whining more than anything.

"It was, but unfortunately it didn't turn out that way. I suspected the contracture, but when I got in there, I realized it was more extensive than I thought. I had to do a full capsulectomy on the left and a partial on the right. The implants were definitely calcified. I thought I might see a little, based on their firmness, but this was more significant than expected. I hadn't anticipated the infection though."

"But why couldn't you have just put the new implants in?"

"Because with the infection, healing will be difficult. Additionally, they are more likely to form excess scar tissue and further capsular contractures. We want that problem to get better, not worse."

I glance down again. "So I have ... nothing?"

"For the time being, you have loose skin. We have to make sure it's in good condition before we try to put new implants in and stretch it out again. We may have to consider smaller implants than before."

"I don't want to be smaller. I liked my proportions the way they were."

"Then perhaps we want to look at a DIEP flap for your next reconstruction."

Next reconstruction.

Those words ricochet through my brain. This isn't over. I have more surgeries ahead.

Crap on a cracker.

Another surgery, though, with the tummy tuck I'd get, it would be a win-win. Or at least a silver lining.

"However, I'm not sure you're a great candidate for it. We will have to see how your healing goes. I'll see you on my rounds tomorrow."

"Tomorrow? I thought this was an outpatient thing. That I could go home."

"Do you feel up to going home?"

Now that he mentions it, no.

"You need to stay here while you're on the IV antibiotics. At least one more day. We'll see tomorrow what the incisions look like."

When the doctor leaves, I try to process everything he's told me, but all I keep coming back to is this:

I have no breasts.

He took my breasts away and didn't give me any in return.

What am I going to tell Mike? He's going to be horrified.

Except he's not horrified. He's pissed. Like *super* mad. But only ... he's mad *at* me.

As if I had anything to do with this. As if it's my fault that the implants were recalled or that my body rejected them or that I have an infection.

"Jesus, Marg, you told me this was going to be easy. I was thinking I could still attend the second half of the conference this weekend. You know, at least get two days in, if not the full four."

"I'm sorry, Mike, that my health is such an inconvenience. Trust me, I am not thrilled with this development either."

"What are you going to do?"

You. Not we. I don't like his tone on this. Not one bit.

"Well, I'm here at least through tomorrow. I can call my mom to come."

"No, Jesus, no."

I look at him for a minute. "If you're still planning on going away, who is going to help me? I don't know if I'm going to have the drains when I go home this time."

"Bailey can help."

"I am not asking our thirteen-year-old to help me with my drain tubes. I don't know what this is going to look like under here, but I know it's not going to be good. It will scar her for life." Looking at it might scar *me* for life. I cannot picture what it will look like.

Mike stands up and pitches his phone down on the bed, pinging me in the leg. "I don't understand why you couldn't have waited, Marg. This is the worst possible timing."

And with that, he storms out.

I'm stunned.

Actually stunned. How can he be upset with me for this? It's not my fault. Nothing I've done could have contributed to nor prevented this. How—

His phone pings with a text notification. Reflexively, I pick it up.

So if you come, I'll come. You always take care of me first.

Then, there are a series of emojis, including several eggplants and a peach.

I've taken enough safe-internet parenting classes to know the sender is not referring to anything found in the produce section.

A wave of nausea hits me, even as I try to open up the phone. My hands shake as I type Mike's super-secret code. 6-4-5-3. It spells Mike, in case you were wondering.

And there it is, laid out in a string of text messages.

Work conference my ass.

That SOB is going to leave me in a hospital bed so he can go shag his mistress.

Okay, I know I'm not British, but the American way to put it sounds so much more vulgar.

Bloody wanker.

How could he have done this? How could he be cheating on me? Why is he cheating on me? I thought he was happy with me. With us. I thought he loved me. What more could I have done to make him happy?

I know he doesn't like my mom, so I don't have her visit us all that much. The only other thing I can think of is this breast cancer–BRCA thing, but it's not like I have control over that.

The house is clean. Food is prepared routinely and expertly. I've kept myself up, practically starving myself to keep the early menopause pounds off. The kids are well mannered. At least they are outside the home. Mike can come and go as he pleases.

I guess I didn't realize how literally he was going to take that.

If I weren't under the influence of some heavy-duty drugs, I'd probably be going on a rage right now.

Not actually in public, where people can see, because that's just not done. But if we were home, man, I'd be screaming.

And throwing things.

And there'd be a whole lot of cursing going on.

I'd have to make sure the kids were out, of course, because I don't want them to see us fighting like that.

Mike comes back in the room. "Oh, there's my phone."

I could hand it to him. I could bean him in the head with it.

The latter seems infinitely more appealing.

"I've got to make some calls."

"I'm sure you do."

He starts to head out of the room. What do I do? What do I say? I've got to say something, even though there are other people around, right?

Maybe it's because I'm drugged up. Maybe it's because I've woken up from a supposedly simple surgery with no breasts. Maybe it's because he's bonking someone else. Whatever the reason, I decide right here and now is the time to say something.

"Hey, Mike, I think you should go to that conference. Why don't you go right now?"

He stops and turns, his mouth agape. "What? You want me to go?"

I try not to notice the hope in his voice. In this moment, I hate him with every fiber of my being. "Yeah, I know this ruined everything, and I didn't mean to inconvenience you. I'll see if Becky can watch the kids until my mom gets here."

"Really? You mean it?"

I can't ignore that he's suddenly become animated and as excited as a puppy.

This only fuels my rage.

I want to say, "No, I don't mean it, you stupid ass. They're your kids. The very least you can do is watch them for a day."

Instead, through gritted teeth, I spit out, "Absolutely. Go home and pack right now. And while you're at it, pack all your shit, because I think when you leave, you should never come back."

"What?"

This is enough to get his attention.

"You heard me. I want you gone. Good-bye. Adios. I get the house, no questions asked. I never want to see you or your cheating ass again."

"Yeah, that's fine." He sags against the doorframe, nonplussed by the bomb I just dropped on him.

"Fine?" My voice is a strangled scream.

"I was going to move out after the holidays, but then this"—he waves his hand at my chest area—"came up. It really messed with my timeline."

"Your timeline?" I feel like all I can do is repeat his last word as he lands blow after blow.

"Yeah, I have a place, but it won't be ready until after the first of the year. I'll send the kids the address when I'm in."

"A place," I repeat. This is a bad dream. Maybe it's part of the anesthesia, and when I wake up, I'll have my new boobs and a faithful husband. Yes, that's it. This is all a bad dream.

CHAPTER 7

This is not a bad dream.

This is my life.

Becky is at the hospital before I can say "my husband is a cheating, lying ass." In all fairness, she was probably on her way over anyway.

"It's over. We've been together about twenty years, and it's done," I say numbly. I need to ask for another round of pain medication. Sure, my chest hurts, but my brain hurts more.

"What am I going to tell the kids? What am I going to tell my mom? What will people think?"

"Knowing you, you will put a positive spin on things so your children don't realize what a dick their father is. You will tell your mother because she's never really liked Mike, and she will agree with you on what a dick he is. And people will think what they want to think. You can't change that."

This is why Becky is my best friend.

I'm trying not to cry. Not because I want to be stoic—even though I desperately do—but because the wracking sobs hurt my chest. The SOB has not only detonated my life but has done so at a time when it's impossible for me to deal with it properly.

Becky sits there, holding my hand. There's so much to say, but neither of us knows where to start. After a long while I say, "I didn't even see this coming."

"Really?" Becky asks. She's pulled back and is looking at me as if I have two heads. Or no boobs.

One of those is true.

"Yes, really. I had no idea. I thought we were solid." Then her words hit me. "Did you know?"

"Well, I didn't know *know*, but I had my suspicions."

"Suspicions? What kind of suspicions? Why didn't you say anything?"

"Um, like the realtor's card. You were so jazzed about the lake house that I didn't want to burst your bubble."

I feel like a fool. Humiliated beyond belief. The thought of the new house had slipped my mind in all the chaos of the holidays and my surgery and the radio humiliation. I'd forgotten all about it, including my plans to order custom signs, which, come to think of it, is not like me at all.

Even on Christmas morning when I opened the sweater from Mike, I didn't remember right away about the house. I ended up getting Mike a tie and a leaf blower because although I *knew* I'd come up with a great gift idea, I couldn't remember what it was or where I'd saved the information.

Normally, I'm like an elephant who remembers everything.

Or at least I used to be before I started missing appointments and forgetting that my husband was supposed to be giving me a lake house for Christmas.

Instead of decorating my dream home, I'm getting a divorce.

The tears well up and run down my face.

"Oh, Marg, I'm so sorry. I don't know what to say. I had a feeling, but I hoped I was wrong."

"You're never wrong about these things. You have an intuition or something. What else are you sitting on that you aren't telling me?"

Becky shrugs. "I don't know. But it's probably going to get worse before it gets better."

Great.

"I'm scared to even ask how. I don't have a husband. I don't have a real job. And I don't have boobs. Oh, and last week, TJ the DJ and Todd awarded me the Jerk-Face Award on Morning Meltdown. I can't even go into UnBRCAble and talk about this and the reasons why my husband started screwing someone else because *he* will be there. Oh, that's right. TJ the DJ is the dude in my UnBRCAble group. But I can't complain because that makes me a jerk-face. Merry freakin' Christmas to me."

"What do you need me to do?"

Again, this is why we're friends.

"Can you take the kids or check in on them or something? Jordan has practices at stupid early hours, and Bailey will stay up all night on her phone. My mom will be here tomorrow."

"She can't make it until tomorrow? Not that I mind. It's no issue whatsoever. It's just odd that she's waiting."

I don't want to get into it, but I don't have the energy to make something up. "She has a facial peel today. Apparently, it had to be timed perfectly between Christmas and New Year's so she looks in tip-top shape for her hot date."

"Isn't she, like, in her seventies?" Becky wrinkles her nose.

"Seventy-four. But she doesn't want to look a day over fifty." Looks are so important to her. It's one of the reasons I've always been a disappointment. My skin was too pale. My nose didn't fit my face. I was chubby before I grew, and then I was too tall. I was always *too* something for her. Too something to be perfect.

No doubt my breasts—or lack thereof—will be disappointing to her as well.

At least she's coming.

"How are you feeling otherwise? Like from the surgery."

I roll my shoulders. "Actually, not bad. I mean, not great, but compared to the original mastectomy and spacers and reconstruction, this is better. I'm not waking up with rocks on my chest."

"What did they tell you about your next surgery?"

"Not much. It'll depend on how quickly the infection clears up and how well I heal. I'll need prayers for that, definitely."

Hell, the way my life is going, I'm going to need all the prayers.

~~~**~~~

I currently hate my husband and everything he stands for, but there is a *slight* possibility he was right about one thing:

Asking my mother to come and stay was a bad idea.

She's like every stereotypical overbearing mother. Except she's mine.

On the plus side, my house is spotless, and my freezer is full of meals.

On the negative side, they are low-fat, low-calorie meals that probably taste like grass and cardboard. Still, in a pinch, they'll do.

It's the thought that counts, really.

Four days after my breasts were removed and my marriage quietly imploded, I'm able to get out of bed and even sit on the couch for a while. This recovery is going much faster than my last two rounds of surgery.

Maybe the drugs are better than they were six years ago.

Maybe it's because I have no choice but to get better quickly. Mom is leaving in the morning, and I'll be on my own with the kids. It's probably a good thing she's driving me nuts, otherwise I'd be tempted to ask her to stay longer.

Not that she would. She has a date tomorrow night for New Year's Eve. I get to stay home with a surly teenager who is upset that I can't drive her all over

God's creation. Jordan has plans to hang with his swim buddies, so he won't be skulking around.

I want to tell Bailey to ask her father to drive her, but he's God-knows-where shacking up with God-knows-who. I assume it's the same woman from the texts, but I also assumed my husband would be faithful to me.

I wonder if he'll be faithful to her or if he'll trade her in for a newer model when her parts start to break down.

"Oh good, you're up. You need to get moving. Put this all behind you. Call your surgeon and get your next surgery scheduled. You can't even think about dating until you get *that* taken care of." Mom waves in the general direction of my chest.

"Dating?" I shake my head as if there might be something in my ears because there's no way I heard that correctly. "I'm still married."

"Yeah, on paper. You need to admit, darling, that that ship has left the port, and you're still standing on the dock. The best thing you can do is get yourself on another ship as soon as possible."

I have a mental image of Indiana Jones swimming to the Nazi ship to save the ark. Knowing me, if I tried to do that, I'd drown.

"I don't think I'm looking to date anytime soon. I mean ..."

"You have to get back on the horse. The longer you sit in the stable—"

Man, my mother does love her metaphors.

"Yes, well, shouldn't I try to figure out what went wrong here before I jump right in again?" Considering that my mom has had one relationship right after another my whole life, and they all end the same way, I *probably* shouldn't heed her advice.

"You can try asking Mike. It's not a bad idea. That way, you know the things you need to change before you try again."

She walks out of the room before I can even formulate a response. I know she's right though. I should have tried harder. Done better. *Been better.* Mike wouldn't have needed to find someone else if I had worked harder.

Maybe if I promise to do better, he'll come ba—

No, wait.

He's screwing someone else. He was cheating on me. For long enough that he made alternative living arrangements. It wasn't as if he was walking and slipped and accidentally put his penis in someone else.

This was no accidental penis slippage.

This was purposeful. Deliberate.

Suddenly, I need answers.

I pick up my phone and call Mike. We haven't spoken in three days, which is the longest we've gone without talking since the day we started dating. I have no idea where he is. The only thing I am certain of is that he's with *her*.

I don't care. He's still my husband, and at the very least he owes me is an explanation.

I hear him sighing as he answers. "Yes?"

I freeze, not knowing what to say.

"Marg, what do you want?" He sounds angry. Like he has any right to be angry with me. I'm the victim here. I'm the one who should be angry.

And damn straight, I am.

"I just want to know why. Why didn't you just leave me? Why did you have to screw someone else? How could you do this to me? To us? To the kids? What in God's name were you thinking?"

"You're a lot to deal with, Marg. All the time."

A lot to deal with? Are you kidding me?

"What's so hard to deal with? The groceries always bought? The house always impeccable? The successful kids? The attractive, smart wife? The time to ski in the winter and golf in the summer? You don't even mow the lawn here! What exactly is so hard?"

"Who do you think works to pay for that? I feel like I can barely sit down in my own house, lest I mess up your throw pillows or make footprints on your freshly vacuumed carpet. It's too much pressure. *You're* too much pressure."

"I'm too much pressure? You're the one who hated if there was even a piece of paper left out on the counter or if there were dishes in the sink. But you didn't do them. You simply complained. So for years— *years*—I ran myself ragged trying to keep the house the way you wanted. And now you're going to justify your infidelity saying I was too intense about the house?"

"Listen, Marg, I don't want to listen to you nag anymore. I don't have to. It's why I left. Now unless it's an issue with the kids, I don't care to talk to you right now."

I'm stunned at his callousness. Sure, he was never a warm and fuzzy type, but I never thought him to be cold and cruel. "Mike, I just had major surgery. I can barely wipe myself, and I'm going to have to go in for more. I need help."

"You're resourceful. I'm sure you'll figure it all out. Or find someone you can nag to death into doing your bidding."

And then he disconnects.

As if *he* has a right to hang up. I want to call him back if only so I can slam the phone down on him.

CHAPTER 8

I stare at the door leading into the UnBRCAble meeting. The main door to the Genevieve T. Wunderlich Women's Health Center has a handicapped accessible switch to automatically open the door.

Apparently the interior doors do not.

I've never noticed before, but since I'm eight days out of surgery, I'm noticing now. Mostly because I'm not cleared to pull the heavy door open yet. With two Wednesday holidays in a row, Claudia had the wherewithal to move the January first meeting to the next day.

I need this group.

But first, I need to figure out how to open the door.

I could wait for someone to come in, but seeing as how I'm already late, I don't know if anyone else is coming.

Yes, I'm late, but I had to Uber here. Hopefully, I get cleared to drive tomorrow. I don't know what I'm going to do otherwise. Jordan is going to have to bite the bullet and get his driver's license.

He wasn't thrilled when I told him that. I remember being sixteen and chomping at the bit to be able to drive—for the freedom it represented. Kids today are different. They're content being chauffeured around, too unmotivated for the work driving entails. I didn't think my kids would be like this, but here we are. Jordan is pushing seventeen and *still* doesn't have his license.

Of course, he probably needs to learn to drive first. Mike was supposed to teach him, but he never got around to it. I need to look into Drivers Ed for him, and I need it to happen fast. Otherwise I'm at the mercy of Uber drivers, so I'll probably never be on time again.

"Is there a reason why you're standing out here, blocking the door?" The voice behind me startles me for a second, before rage and indignation fill me.

I whirl around. There's that stupid lollipop sticking out of his mouth again. I don't understand it. He's like some overgrown child. "You're TJ the DJ. Why didn't you say something before?"

"I told you I was in radio. I just don't want people to get crazy attached to me. When I meet people through my personal life, I want to keep them in that section of my life. If I tell them who I am, that line gets blurred. "

"I call bull. If you wanted to keep them separate, you wouldn't have been blabbing all over the radio about how I offended you. You called me a jerk-face!" I pull my puffy coat tighter. This is the first time I've ventured out in public. At least it's winter, so I can layer up and no one can see how horribly disfigured I am.

"Oh, you heard that?"

"You don't keep your lives separate. It's not fair and an invasion of my privacy!" My voice is louder than I intend, but I can't seem to control it.

The door swings open. It's Millie. "Everything okay out here? Oh, Marg! I didn't know if you'd make it tonight. Are you okay?"

"Thank you," I say curtly as I walk in. It never even occurred to Thom or TJ or whatever his name is to open the door for me. I realize in my haste to get away from him I'm being rude to Millie. I lower my voice so he can't hear me. "Thanks for the door. I can't pull it open yet. Hopefully tomorrow."

"I remember those days. I've always wondered why this office suite doesn't have automatic doors," Millie says.

I take my coat off gingerly, though I'm feeling better than I had expected. Definitely better than the first go 'round with this. It's not as hard to move. I don't have the drains in either, which makes a big difference. Even so, I have to be careful about where I sit. Tonight, I'll have no choice but to sit in the elevated chair with sturdy wooden armrests and a padded back.

Otherwise known as the surgery seat.

There's an unspoken rule that it is saved for whoever has just gone under the knife.

Except the moment I cross the room to sit there, Thom plops down in the seat. He's removed his jacket to reveal a Hawaiian shirt with Snoopy as Joe Cool all over it. Casually, he twirls the lollipop stick.

This shirt is not as heinous as some of his others, but certainly nothing to be proud of.

He's sitting in the surgery seat.

"Can you please move?" I ask through gritted teeth, though I want to scream at him. That wouldn't be the polite thing to do. I also want to shove that stick somewhere very impolite as well.

"Why?"

"I'd like to sit there." No, that's not strong enough. "I need to sit there ... please." The last word may have come out as more of a growl than a request.

Millie hustles over. "Oh, yes, Thom. You're new here. That seat is reserved for anyone just out of surgery. It's easier to get in and out of."

I think I see the beast's face color a bit. "Oh, sorry." He stands up. "I didn't know."

I sit down a little too forcefully and wince slightly. Claudia looks at me. "How are you feeling, Marg? How did everything go?"

Before I can control it, tears well up. No, I will not cry here. I blink them back rapidly. "Um, not great." I'm staring at my French manicure rather than looking at the sympathetic gazes of the rest of the members. If I see those looks, I'll have a full-on meltdown. "But enough about me. Did everyone have a good holiday?" My voice is strained and unusually high.

Millie glances at me nervously and then to Erin. "Um, it was great. Piper was thrilled with the bedroom makeover we did for her. Nine going on nineteen is such a hard age, but she feels like a teenager now."

Frances, Tracey, and Kelli all talk about their holidays and how great everything was. "I even had a date for New Year's for the first time in ages. I'd forgotten how great it is to be able to kiss someone at midnight!" Tracey gushes.

I may never kiss anyone at midnight again.

Ever.

And with that, the tears I'd been so desperate to suppress burst forth as a guttural sound emanates from deep within my chest. All eyes swivel to me immediately.

"Mike ... left ... girlfriend ... cheater," I manage to say through sobs. "I'm all alone!" I wail.

The ladies in the group offer their condolences and outrage.

"Oh no!"

"I can't believe it!"

"That bastard!"

The only person who is silent is Thom, which is good. I am feeling a generalized anger toward all members of the male species right now, so I'd be happy to aim my cannons at him.

Claudia, the ever-calm voice of reason, asks, "Marg, when did this happen?"

Since I've got no strength left to be strong, I crumble. "Right after I woke up from surgery to find out that it was much more complicated than expected."

"Oh no. What were the complications?"

"The worst. I had capsular contractures and calcifications. Dr. Chung had to do a full capsulectomy on the left and a partial on the right. Additionally, the left side was infected. I had to stay in overnight while I got IV antibiotics. I had drains again, but at least those came out the day after. I didn't have to go home with them."

Kelli's hands fly to her mouth. She's yet to have any surgeries, so she doesn't know what fun and joy this is. "But they were able to put the replacements in, right?"

I don't need to answer because my hung head says it all.

"When?" Claudia asks.

I shrug. It doesn't hurt to do that anymore. "I have a follow-up tomorrow, so I'll find out then. From what I hear, at least three months, but it could be as long as six, and then I'll have to do spacers. Again."

The thought of having to go through all that again hits me like a ton of bricks. At least last time, I had Mike and my mom to help me. There were lots of mom friends who pitched in, and Becky was like my right hand.

This time, all I will have is Becky, most likely. I think my mom will come. Maybe. Jordan will definitely have to be driving before I can schedule this. Unfortunately, I may have to ask my kids to help me, though I loathe the idea. But that's putting the cart before the horse.

Erin waves her hands. "Wait, hold up! What happened with Mike? I just saw you guys a few weeks ago at Millie's wedding. How? What? Why?"

I recap how Mike was upset at my surgical results and his error in leaving his phone on my bed. "The fact is, he was planning on leaving me anyway. He is moving into his new place today. They were planning on having a holiday ski trip between Christmas and New Year's. He told me it was a work conference. I have a feeling a lot of his late-night meetings have not actually been work related."

I see Millie's lips tense.

"Millie, did you know?" I ask. She's not a close friend. Not one who owed me anything enough to tell me. Still, if she knew, she should have said something. Hos before bros. Wait, that's not right. Sisters before misters.

That's better.

She shakes her head. "No, but I thought it a little odd that he worked such long hours. Sterling is always out the door promptly at five thirty, but I thought maybe Mike had more responsibility or something."

I put my head in my hands. "You know, the week after your wedding, he told me he had to work late each night because Sterling was on his honeymoon. When I saw you here, I chalked it up to the holidays and figured Mike was Christmas shopping for me. Even when I found the business card from a realtor, I—"

"Wait, hold up." Thom pulls the stick out of his mouth, waves his hands, and makes a *T* with them. "Time out. Are you telling me that your husband never came home from work on time, lied about where he was, and had a business card from a realtor, and you didn't suspect anything? Listen, I don't know you well, but are you really that stupid?"

Apparently I am.

"I'm sure it was obvious to everyone but me. I feel like a fool. I don't need you to point it out. Hindsight is twenty-twenty. I've been with Mike for almost half my life. It never occurred to me that he would do this. That he *could* do this. I thought we had the perfect life."

"Nobody's life is perfect."

"Well, mine was until ..." I break off. I don't know when it went wrong. I don't know why. I don't want to believe Mike's cock-and-bull story that I nag too much, but I must have done something to drive him away.

A long-buried memory of my parents fighting bobs into my conscious thought. It wasn't long before my dad left. I can still hear his words, ricocheting through my brain.

You're going to have to do better if you ever want someone to love you.

I'm not sure what I did, but obviously I should have done better.

CHAPTER 9

As the UnBRCAble meeting draws to a close, Millie approaches me. "Marg, I'm so sorry. Do you need anything? Anything at all?"

I'm a helper, not a helpee. "I'm good. Thanks."

I walk with her out to the parking lot into the frigid January air, searching for my keys. Only when I pull them out do I remember that I didn't drive here. I've got to call an Uber to get home.

Crap on a cracker.

"Actually, Millie, do you think there's any way you could give me a lift home? I can't drive yet." I don't know why I ask. It's unnecessary. I don't know her that well. Certainly not well enough to put her out like that.

"Oh, gosh, I'm so sorry, Marg, but I can't. I'm late to Piper's winter concert as it is."

I wave off the rejection, which is stinging much more than it should. "No worries. I shouldn't have asked. I'll get an Uber."

"I can drive you." The deep, raspy timbre of the voice can only belong to one person here.

"No thank you, Thom." I begin walking back toward the main entrance. I will wait inside until my Uber comes.

"Come on. Don't waste your money. I can drive you home. It's no big deal. It's not like I have anyone waiting at home for me either."

I stop and stare at him, cruising along behind me in his car. It's straight out of the 1970s and is probably making up for something that's lacking elsewhere. "You have such a gift for words. I wonder how you became employed in the first place."

He waggles his eyebrows. "Wouldn't you like to know?"

Yuck. "Actually, no, but it is quite cold out here and okay, fine. You can take me home."

"Yes, your majesty."

I walk around the front of the red car and see from the front grill that it's an Oldsmobile. Hawaiian shirts and this car. He really must be compensating for something.

I'm surprised he doesn't have a Magnum, P.I. mustache and cigar.

When I get to the passenger's side and attempt to pull the door open, I realize it must be made of lead. A shot of pain rips through my chest, from my right armpit to the middle of where my breast used to be. I gasp, gripping my chest with my left hand.

"On second thought, maybe this isn't a good idea," I say.

The window is up on this side of the car, and Thom looks at me like I'm crazy. A little louder I say, "I can't pull this open."

He cups his hand to his ear, indicating he has no idea what I'm saying.

"I CAN'T OPEN THE DOOR. I NEED HELP," I yell.

I see Thom throw the stick shift into park and open the door. As he walks around the front of the car, he says over the loud engine, "This had better not be a ploy to get me to be at your beck and call. I'm not the chivalrous type." He yanks the door open. With this vintage car, I expected a big bench, so I'm relieved to see the bucket seats.

It takes me a minute to get the seatbelt and fasten it across my body. Thom's back in on his side and looking at me like I have six heads.

"What?" I snap. I'm all out of patience.

"Why can't you move or open your door? You're really not that much of a princess, are you?"

I sigh. It's not his fault he's an ignorant man. I could stay mad at him for being ignorant or I can help him be less of an ass. I sigh again. "Alright, but this is not radio material."

"Everything in my life is radio material. It's what I do."

I glare at him.

"Okay, fine. You get this one exemption. This will not end up on the radio."

"My implants were under the muscle."

He looks at me blankly.

"Just go. I'll explain while you're driving." I give him my address, which he promptly types into his phone navigator. Then I continue. "With a mastectomy, they take out all your br ... breast tissue. Scrape it out, like the inside of a melon."

I really hate that analogy, but it seems to work best.

"So all you have is a sack of skin over your pectoralis muscle. There's nothing to hold the implant in place. So, many times, they slide it under the pectoralis muscle. You with me so far?"

He glances at me out of the corner of his eye. "Got it."

"My implants were recalled because they can cause cancer, which defeats the point of them, really. But even before that and unbeknownst to me, my body was reacting to them. It's called a capsular contracture. This ..." I stop for a minute. I'm about to get deeply personal with someone I don't know.

On the other hand, I'm in his car and pretty much helpless. It seems I've already given up using wise judgment.

"My body formed hard, thick scar tissue around the implants. The doctor had to remove this capsule that formed too. It's all under the pec muscles, so they are quite sore." Though if I think about it, they're not as painful as they had been. I'm healing much quicker this time around.

I see Thom wrinkle his nose. "That's kind of gross."

"There's a lot about this that's kind of gross. But what choice do I have? It was go through this or develop a recurrence of my breast cancer. Or ovarian cancer, which because there's no good screening for, they probably wouldn't find until it's too late." I resent having to explain this to him. It's why he doesn't belong in the group. "Things you don't have to worry about."

"Right. I have no worries. No worries at all." The sarcasm drips from his voice. "My body is immune to cancer."

"Less than one percent of breast cancer occurs in males!" I defend. Once you find out you carry a genetic mutation like this, you become very versed in statistics.

"Yes, but my chances of being that one percent are high. Additionally, I have a one in eight chance of developing a very aggressive form of prostate cancer, which *actually* puts me at a higher risk than you for having a fatal cancer. Not to mention pancreatic cancer, which we all know the odds on that one. Oh, also melanoma and colon cancer. But please, tell me again how I don't have to worry."

"You don't have to get snippy with me. You told me I was gross."

"I did not say you were gross. I said the capsular thingy, whatever it's called, sounded gross. Sometimes the human body is gross. Haven't you ever watched Dr. Pimple Popper?"

I ignore his attempt to deflect with humor. This is not a laughing matter. "It's the same thing. And this—*this*—is why I don't want you in the group. You can't possibly understand what it's like. Call me a jerk-face all you want. I need a safe space where I can talk, and with you there, I'm not safe to say what I'm going through without you calling me gross and—oh shit."

We've pulled up in front of the house, and Mike's car is there. Which means Mike is there.

"Son of a—just when I thought this night couldn't get any worse," I mutter as Thom turns into the driveway. He looks at me, and I stare back.

"What?" he asks.

"Still can't open the door. Those pec muscles haven't magically healed on the seven-minute drive home." My frustration comes flying out of my mouth. "Sorry. Oh my God, I'm so sorry. I didn't mean to say that out loud. I … I'm not usually like this. I'm sorry."

Maybe I should add in another "sorry."

Thom laughs. "I'll take your word for it. Bear with me, I forgot. I'm a slow learner."

"I'm sorry." I have to be more patient, but I have no spoons left for being polite. Especially not with Mike here.

Mike stole my last spoon.

Still, that's no excuse for abusing Thom like this.

He rolls his eyes again before getting out and coming around to my side of the car. As I'm getting out, I see the porch light flick on, and Mike is illuminated as he walks outside.

"What the hell is that car? It's violating the noise ordinance in the neighborhood. I should call the cops!" Mike yells from the porch.

You know, also violating the noise ordinance.

Which, actually, doesn't go into effect until 9:00 p.m.

Thom looks at me. "No wonder you're in a perpetual bad mood. I'd be miserable too if I had to deal with that douche. Listen to me. No matter what he says, cut your losses and run. Do not take him back."

I glance from my husband to this man I barely know. "That's an awful quick assessment of his character, don't you think?"

"Trust me. I can read people. He's an ass, and if you stay with him, you are too."

I brush past him. "Good to know that if I'm going to be an ass, at least I'll be a gross ass. Thank you for the ride."

"Marg, listen," he grabs my arm. "All I'm saying is you deserve better. Don't settle."

~~~***~~~

Play it cool. Play it cool. Don't let Mike know what a mess you've been.

"I didn't expect to see you here tonight. Did you want to talk?" That was totally cool. I won't even make him ask to talk. I won't make him grovel. Well, maybe a little.

"No, I thought you'd be gone. I'm here to get some more of my stuff."

And when he says some more of his stuff, he means most of the furniture in the den, as well as the kitchen table and the barstools at the kitchen counter.

"Where's my furniture?" I demand.

"Your furniture?" he mocks.

"Yes," I scream, waving my arms. "The furniture that I picked out and bought because you were too busy to look!" That goes for the kitchen stuff. The den was all his doing.

"The furniture you bought, and I paid for. It's mine."

I open my mouth, but no words come out.

"You look like you're catching flies."

That snaps my mouth shut. "But, Mike, you can't take the furniture. What am I going to sit on to eat?"

He laughs. "Like you ever actually eat. God, you've got problems. Serious problems." He picks up a box and shakes his head. "I don't know how I managed to stay with you for as long as I did. Man, I felt dead inside. This past week has been such a relief, not being around you. I feel so alive."

With his words, part of me dies. Tears fill my eyes and spill out, hot and salty as they pour down my face. I don't understand how he can say these things. I don't understand what I did to deserve his harsh words. "Mike, I ..."

He holds up a hand, balancing the box on his hip with the other arm. "Don't, Marg. There's nothing you can say."

Huh?

"Nothing I can say what?" I'm pretty sure I deserve the chance to tell him he's being a cruel ass and I never want to see him again, which is how I'm feeling this very second.

"Marg, there is nothing you can say that will make me want to get back together with you. I'm in love with Emily. I'm not in love with you, and I haven't been for a while. Frankly, I haven't even liked you in a while. You're pretty miserable, and you held me to an impossible standard. I got tired of trying to be perfect for you. It's too hard, and I'm not doing it anymore."

And he walks out the door without even giving me the chance to tell him I'd rather lick the bottom of my shoe than kiss him again.

Still, as the door slams, the noise ricochets through me, shattering my heart all over again.

I'm not sure I'll ever get over this.

CHAPTER 10

Trying to be perfect for me. *For me.*

Of all the cockamamie things. He was the one who was so anal retentive about every little detail, like what foods were allowed to be served together and what condiments were appropriate. So sue me if I like ketchup on my bratwurst rather than mustard. In all honesty, I hate mustard.

The food and the color.

So, in reality, I wasn't so sad to see that he took the den furniture, which was mustard yellow. He called it ochre to be fancy, but it was ugly-ass mustard yellow.

Good riddance to him and his condiment-colored couch.

On the other hand, it's going to get annoying real fast now that there's nowhere to sit when we eat. There's a folding card table and chairs out in the garage. It's not great, but it will do in the interim.

I head out to the garage only to remember that I can't carry anything. I'll be so relieved when Dr. Chung tells me I can use my arms again. It's hard enough to be on my own. I certainly can't do it without any arms.

The rage I'm feeling toward Mike dissolves into sadness as I sit down abruptly on the step to the garage. How did this happen? Where—and when—did things go wrong, and how did I not notice?

I'm still sitting there, sobbing, when Bailey emerges from her room, phone in hand. It's not until she gets into the kitchen does she finally look up from her screen.

"What the hell? Why is the door to the garage open?"

"Bailey, watch your language," I admonish, trying to wipe the tears so she won't see them.

"Where's all our stuff?"

"Your father took it to his new place."

"Well, that sucks. Where are we going to eat now? Can I take my food up to my room?"

I sigh, standing gingerly. "No. I've told you, no food in your bedroom. I'm going to have Jordan bring the card table in from the garage."

"Eew. That's going to look bad." Bailey wrinkles her nose at me as if I'm the reason our house is about to look as if it had been designed by a frat boy.

I want to tell her that we'll get a new one soon, but truth be told, I don't know that we will. My few hours a week as a bookkeeper don't pay enough to buy our groceries, let alone keep us in our lifestyle.

My God, what if Mike wants me to buy him out of the house? What if I can't find a job? What about health insurance and college and my car and ...

I feel light-headed. I lie down on the floor, pressing my cheek into the cool tile.

"Mom, what are you doing? It's gross down there. It hasn't been cleaned since Gam left."

Of course it hasn't.

Yet somehow, right now, I don't care. I can't care. I may never get off this floor again. How has everything gone to hell so quickly? I thought I had the perfect life. I thought I had the perfect husband and the perfect children. Well, they're teens, so no one's perfect during those years.

The only thing I have is being a perfect fool.

My stomach is filled with lead, and there's a brick in my throat making it hard to swallow. Thoughts assault and overwhelm me. No matter what I do, I can't stop the barrage.

There are so many questions, none of which I have the answers to. I suspect the answers will not be easily found as well. There are too many variables right now.

"Mom, are you getting up?" Bailey crouches low next to me. It reminds me of how she used to squat to examine bugs in the backyard when she was young. She's not that little girl anymore, but I don't want to do anything to take away from whatever childhood innocence she may have left.

"Yeah, baby." I push myself up gingerly. I have to use my arms to do it. It twinges but isn't painful like I expect it to be. A small silver lining in a really dark, deep cloud. "Just needed a minute to think."

"How long have you been on the floor?"

I glance at the clock. It's been two hours.

And I could easily stay there for two months with the way I'm currently feeling. But I won't because I see the worry in Bailey's eyes. I remember how it was when my father left. Not to mention every man after that.

She needs me to be strong.

I won't make her be strong for me, the way Mom did. As long as I can remember, I've been shouldering a lot of responsibility. More than I should have. I won't do that to her or Jordan. They deserve to be kids.

I stand up and brush myself off. "I'm sorry you had to see that, baby. Obviously things are a little rough right now, but I'll figure things out with your dad, so you don't have to worry about anything."

She looks at me for a beat before turning away. "'Kay."

Alone for a minute, I know I need to do something to make the kitchen work for us. "Jordan," I call. "Can you please come help me?"

I call three more times, each progressively louder before I finally walk up the stairs and knock on the door to his room. He's lying on his bed, large headphones on, looking like he belongs out on an airport tarmac.

"Hey!" I yell, this time waving my hands.

He slides the headphones off. "Yeah?"

"Can you move the card table and chairs in from the garage to the kitchen?"

He rolls his eyes. "I already helped Dad with all his furniture. I'm tired. I don't want to move anything else."

"You *helped* Dad move *his* furniture? *His furniture?*"

"Yeah, the stuff in the den and the kitchen. His clothes and closet stuff too."

I think I'm going to be sick.

"Well, if you ever want to sit to eat again, I need you to move the card table and chairs in."

He shrugs. "I'm not home that much for meals anyway."

"Excuse me?"

Instead of answering, he slides his headset back over his ears and taps his phone screen a few times. From the expression on his face, I know he's now tuned me out. I want nothing more than to scream at him, asking for a *third* time to bring the table in.

But that would be nagging.

So I bite my tongue and back out of Jordan's room, closing his door without him even looking up. While I'm furious with Mike for sneaking in to move his stuff out, I'm hurt that Jordan helped him. Mike may blame me for the end of our marriage, but his behavior is inexcusable.

He's acting like a massive ass.

And maybe I was demanding and asked a lot of him, but it was no more than he asked of me. I'm not the one cheating.

Still, it's a shock to see his side of the closet empty. There is random crap strewn about. It looks as if a bomb went off in here.

What annoys me most in this moment is not that Mike's gone. Hell, if he were here right now, I'd throw him out. It's that I can't pick up and clean and right the messes he's made.

He really is a slob.

At least I won't have to deal with that anymore. No more dirty socks on the floor. No more dental picks on the coffee table. *Used* dental picks, mind you.

Gross.

No more dirty dishes stacked *next to* the sink to let the food congeal and solidify on them. No more candy wrappers balled up and left for the maid to pick up.

For the record, we don't have a maid.

In all the years we've been married, I've never been able to change these habits of Mike's. No matter how I asked, begged, and yes, even nagged, he was unwilling to extend a basic amount of decency and pitch in. When I had my hysterectomy and mastectomy, he hired a weekly cleaner rather than help out.

Then, standing in my closet that looks like a war zone, I start to laugh.

He's Emily's problem now.

Good riddance.

CHAPTER 11

"Are you ready?" Dr. Chung asks expectantly.

"If I say no, will you make it all go away? Oh wait, you already did that."

Without waiting for me to actually be ready, Dr. Chung opens the front of my surgical bra and removes the gauze bandages.

"Margot, open your eyes." No matter how many times I've asked him to call me Marg, he insists on using my full name.

I shake my head, squeezing my eyes shut even harder. I don't want to see the grotesqueness that he's revealed.

That I am.

That is where my breasts used to be.

"Margot, I know this is difficult, but I need you to see what I'm talking about so we can discuss your options."

I open my eyes but look straight ahead, not allowing my gaze to dip down at all. See? I can do this.

The nurse hands me a mirror. Traitor.

"As you know, your skin is very thin. Without the underlying breast tissue to provide nerve and blood supplies, it does not heal well. However, these incisions look beautiful. No sign of residual or recurrent infection, which is great. No tissue death yet."

Yet.

The word that hangs over every mastectomy patient like a guillotine blade suspended from a frayed rope.

"So when can I have my reconstruction?" I ask, finally looking in the mirror for the briefest of seconds. It's enough to see the skin hanging like a pair of socks, my nipples pulling down like pendulums.

I squeeze my eyes shut again, but the image remains, burned in my brain.

"Margot, I know this is hard. You need to know this is one step on the journey. You are not at the finish line yet. This is not how it will be."

Because I trust Dr. Chung, I open my eyes. "Tell me what the journey is."

"You have three options. In about six months, we can put in tissue expanders again. After about three months with those, we can put in another set of implants. See how that goes."

"What do you mean, 'see how that goes'? Shouldn't you know if it's going to work?"

Dr. Chung chuckles. *Chuckles.* "Oh come on, Margot, you know there are no guarantees."

Obviously. Otherwise I wouldn't be sitting here in the first place.

"What are my other options?"

He starts peering at my side, reaching out to touch my waist. "We can look at flap reconstruction, where we harvest skin and blood supply from your abdomen as well as your own fat tissue to construct new breasts."

"A TRAM flap or a DIEP flap?" I want him to know I do my research.

"DIEP would be optimal as it doesn't involve cutting into any muscles. Your body has had enough trauma with the capsular contractures and chronic infection, so my choice would be a DIEP, if possible. I'm not sure you have quite enough fatty tissue, so you will need to gain somewhere between five and ten pounds before the surgery."

It won't be hard physically to do that, but mentally? *Sigh.* I've worked so hard for so long *not* to put on weight, especially with my surgically induced menopause.

"What's the third option?" Maybe it won't involve me getting fat.

Large Marge.

"You do not opt for reconstruction. There'd still be one more procedure to remove excess skin and clean things up aesthetically, of course. We can't leave you hanging." He smiles at his own joke.

My gaze darts down to where I'm literally hanging. I do not find him funny. "So what do you do with all of this"—I wave my hand in front of my deformity—"if you are not reconstructing?" I cannot for the life of me picture what he's talking about.

"Remove the skin and nipples. You'd have a horizontal scar running across. A lot of women who opt for staying flat get very creative with the tattoos in that region. Quite stunning."

My brain is slowly processing what he's saying. Or at least it's trying to. "Wait. Flat?"

He nods, pulling my gown closed before stepping back. "If you don't feel like risking it again with another reconstruction, you can always go flat. About forty percent of women chose to stay flat after mastectomy. It's quite common."

I don't know where he's getting that number from, but no one in the group is flat. He must be mistaken.

Flat.

As if I would ever.

"That's a hard pass for me. Can we schedule my reconstruction now?"

Dr. Chung goes over to his computer and starts typing away. "We've got time. Right now, you need to focus on healing. Keep an eye on your incisions and let me know if anything doesn't seem right. You can drive again and do light work around the house. Don't overdo it, but you can be active. Light exercise. I'll see you in two weeks."

And then he leaves the room.

Quickly, I fasten the front of my surgical bra, tucking my empty bags of skin in. I can't believe I'm going to have to deal with this for six more months. I won't be able to look in the mirror at all.

Once dressed, I head out to the waiting room, where Becky is reading a magazine.

"I'm cleared to drive. I can go back to my life, though I don't know what I'm going back to. I can't get new implants for six months."

I don't bother mentioning the other options. I need to do more research about the DIEP flap reconstruction, but I don't know how I'd manage the recovery without help.

And the third option is so ridiculous, I won't even entertain it.

"Thank you for the ride."

"Want to get a coffee or something? Are you up for it?"

Physically, I am, but emotionally, I'm drained. I have so many things to do: find a lawyer, find a job, find a place to sit in my kitchen.

I also want desperately to not do any of these things. To not *have* to do them.

"Coffee sounds great. My treat. It's the very least I can do."

We pull into Starbucks, and I hesitantly, but independently, open the car door. Of course, the door of Becky's Audi does not weigh three tons like that behemoth antique car that Thom drives. I bet his car doesn't even have power steering.

Still, out of an abundance of caution, I use the handicapped button to open the door. Even though there's no implant straining against my poorly vascularized breast tissue, I'm still worried about the skin dying and my nipples falling off.

In other words, a typical day for a breast cancer thriver.

Once we have our beverages and are sitting, I don't know where to start sorting out the mess that my life has become.

"How are the kids doing with this?"

I shrug. "Hard to tell. Other than the inconveniences of not having a place to sit while eating this morning, they haven't really reacted. I think Bailey is happy she could eat in her room for the time being. She'd be happy if we never got a table again, then she wouldn't have to put her phone down ever."

I think about last night and shrug. "I mean, she did seem somewhat concerned that I lay on the floor and cried for a few hours. But maybe she was just concerned because no one has swept or vacuumed the floor since my mom left three days ago, and Bailey's not used to seeing that kind of dirt in the house."

"Time for the kids to step up."

"I know, but I don't want this to negatively affect them," I say, thinking back to my own tumultuous childhood. Mom was married three times by the time I went to college. Each time her marriage failed, it sent me into a tailspin. The worst, of course, was when Dad left.

Not that their marriage was good. Not even close. But he was my father, and he was supposed to love us.

Supposed to.

"I have to make sure they are okay throughout all of this. That's my first priority. I was not, and well ... you know how that turned out."

It's awesome when your life implodes during the most difficult time of childhood. Though I was eight, I had to grow up fast and quick. Mom was a mess, as usual, and my brother Arlo was a handful. He was only five and rambunctious as all get out. But he was a boy—a boy's boy—and Dad loved that. He didn't know what to do with me. He couldn't understand why I didn't like fishing and camping and all that outdoorsy stuff.

Arlo, of course, reveled in filth until it flaked off of him like Pig Pen.

I still don't like to be dirty.

I know I disappointed Dad simply by being a girl. Also, because I was like Mom, whom he couldn't stand. That's a large cross to bear for a child of any age.

"I don't want Mike to forget about the kids the way my dad seemed to forget about us." Me, really, as he always stayed in better touch with Arlo. Of course, Arlo had football and lacrosse games for my dad to periodically attend. It's not like he was going to show up at my math league contests or French club exhibitions.

"Has he said anything about seeing the kids or visitation?"

I shake my head. "He came over last night when he knew I'd be at UnBRCAble to move stuff out. He made Jordan help him." Or had Jordan willingly volunteered? I can't remember the last time my son offered to help without me asking. Multiple times.

Maybe Jordan wants out too.

"What if the kids want to go live with him? What if they don't want to be near me either?"

Becky scoffs. "Don't be ridiculous, Marg. Those kids would be lost without you. Frankly, Mike is going to be too. He can't even go to the grocery store without calling you three times to find the Pop-Tarts."

This is true. He cannot remember that they are in the cereal aisle and insists they should be with pastries since they are labeled "breakfast pastries."

He's an idiot.

"I don't know where he's even living, or if it's in the school district or not. The kids may have to stay with me, at least during the week. Mike did the bare minimum with shuttling the kids back and forth to begin with. I can't imagine him picking up the slack now. Though, depending on what I do for work, I might need him to."

I mull it over for a minute. "If I get a job during the day, I might still be able to drop the kids off at school, but there's no way I can pick them up. They'll have to take the bus home." I look down at my coffee cup. "Damn, I'm changing their lives already."

"You aren't changing them. Mike is. This is not on you."

I appreciate my friend saying that.

My father left because he couldn't stand my mother. Couldn't handle her free-spiritedness. He wanted more. More structure. More organization. More perfection. I gave Mike all that, and it still wasn't enough.

I have no more to give.

CHAPTER 12

Thank God it's winter.

Normally I hate the bulk layers add to my frame, but right now I revel in the protection and padding they supply. Flowing tops, sweaters, and the ever-present scarf around my neck help to camouflage the fact that my D-cups are now AAs, loose tissue squashed into a sports bra. It would be a totally great solution if not for the hot flashes.

I may be wearing turtlenecks until I have my reconstruction.

That's only when I venture out, which isn't often. I don't consider chauffeuring my kids to and fro going out, and my oversized hoodie from a family vacation in the Outer Banks covers enough most days.

Actually, it was Mike's hoodie. Normally I would never be caught dead in something so baggy and unflattering. Now I relish in its shapelessness. And he left it behind, just as he left his family behind.

Just as he left *me* behind.

I think he texts with the kids. Jordan at least, to check in on his swim times, not that he's been to a meet since he left us two weeks ago.

Me.

He left me.

The kids are an unintended casualty. They will pay the price because I wasn't a good enough wife.

By failing in that capacity, I also failed as a mother.

Just as I failed as a daughter.

I'm sensing a theme.

But today, I need to dust myself off and brush away those feelings of inadequacy, no matter how numerous they may be.

I have a job interview.

Mike is still making house and car payments and depositing money into the account for food and such for the kids. That's what the paperwork from his lawyer says.

At least he's not being a dick about that.

I need to find a lawyer. I mentally add it to the ever-growing list of things I need to figure out. I've been putting that off because from what I gather, lawyers like to be paid. The nonprofit company for which I do bookkeeping cannot afford to increase my hours, and that measly salary won't pay my bills.

While I like working with numbers, as there's nothing so satisfying as when a column totals up perfectly, I'm willing to consider lots of things, as long as they pay.

This job happens to be in central administration of my kids' school district. It's a year-round position, but I don't think the kids will need me home during the summer as they have in the past.

Also, it's not like I have a choice anymore.

"Mrs. Kensington, so nice to see you again." I'm greeted warmly by the superintendent, with whom I'd had many dealings during my multiple tenure on the PTO board. He gestures for me to sit opposite him at the conference table in his office.

My nerves jangle as if they're bacon frying in a pan. I haven't been on a job interview in years—since before Jordan was born.

Forget years, it's more like decades.

I sit in uncomfortable silence as Mr. Johannson reads through my application. He slides his readers down slightly and looks up at me. "You were interested in the position in the registrar's office?"

I don't like his use of past tense. I nod, trying to swallow this massive lump in my throat. "Yes," I finally manage to croak. "Now that the kids are older, it makes sense to re-enter the workforce in a larger capacity. As you can see, I've been working for PennHAA for years."

"PennHAA?"

"Yes, the Pennsylvania Housing for Aging Adults. It's a nonprofit that helps seniors downsize and get into subsidized housing. I worked for them full-time before the kids, and I've been their bookkeeper ever since. Quite an impressive tenure. You don't often see people stick with one employer for twenty years."

He glances at the resume again, this time tilting his head back to look through the readers balanced precariously on the end of his nose. "Yes, but that's all you've done."

All I've done?

It sounds like something Mike would say to me. I swallow the words that threaten to bubble out. "As I'm sure you are aware, raising children is a full-time job. Additionally, I've held every position on the PTO board at least once. I've chaired the book fair and raffle basket fundraiser eight consecutive years at Quaker Road Elementary. I did the QRE yearbook and organized the sixth-grade graduation dance both years my children were graduating. Surely those years of service and organization, to the benefit of the school, count for something."

Mr. Johannson shifts slightly. "Yes, but you haven't worked in a school setting before. The registrar's office is one of our most busy departments, especially with the upcoming kindergarten registration."

Crap.

I need this job. I need to play it cool.

"Right. But as you know, I am prompt, organized, and efficient. I can learn quickly and—"

He stands up. "Okay, so we'll be in touch soon."

I'm being dismissed. This certainly doesn't bode well for being hired. I can't walk out of here with everyone knowing I was interviewed and passed over.

"Mr. Johannson, I've worked for the past eleven years to make this school district a wonderful, enriched community. I'm an asset wherever I go, and this office would be lucky to have me."

He nods slowly. "Maybe so. Someone will be in touch."

No. No. No. No. *NO.*

"But I ..."

"Good-bye, Marg." He herds me toward his door. I'm barely through it when it closes behind me with an unusually loud thud.

I will not cry in public. I will not cry in public. *I will not*—dammit.

Hurriedly, and even though I'm inside, I pull my sunglasses down and rush out of the office. I rip off the visitor's badge stuck to my chest and slap it on the front desk before exiting the building. A rush of cold January air hits my face, threatening to freeze the tears in place.

I'm a failure at everything I've ever tried.

This is not how I saw my life going.

Not in the least.

~~~**✱✱**~~~

Six interviews. Zero job offers.

It's like life just keeps kicking me while I'm down.

Who knew leaving the workforce to raise your children was a cardinal sin? Probably the people who knew that keeping a well-run house and staying attractive for your husband was also a cardinal sin.

I don't have to worry about that now.

I look around at the dishes piled up and the overflowing trash. My sweatshirt has coffee stains down the front of it, and it's been at least three days since I've showered.

"Mom?" Bailey walks in. I didn't realize she was even home.

"In here."

"You're still in bed?" The disdain drips from her voice.

"Yeah. What else do I have to do? There's not a lot of reason to get up."

"Um, picking me up from school for starters."

Shit.

"What time is it?" I struggle to sit up and look at the clock. Yup, it's past the time I was supposed to pick Bailey up.

"I called you. You didn't answer."

I look at my phone, the battery drained dead from playing Gardenscapes. I'd been too lazy to get up and charge it. "Sorry. Phone died," I offer unapologetically.

"I had to call Dad. He was super pissed. He said he's gonna call his lawyer."

Let him. It's not like I have anything for him to take, as the last communication from his mouthpiece reminded me. I have three months to buy him out of the car lease and to get a job that has health insurance for myself. He mentioned putting the house on the market and splitting the proceeds fifty-fifty. I don't want the kids to have to move right now, so I'm fighting that. I'd get about twenty percent of the joint assets (generous, in his terms) and none of his retirement if I agree.

I may not have a law degree, but even I know it's a crap arrangement. And what he's offering in child support will barely cover the food bill for two teens, let alone their extracurricular expenses and phone bills.

"That's fantastic news. What else did he have to say on the way home?"

Bailey folds her arms and juts her chin out. "Nothing. He didn't pick me up. He told me to take the late bus. Do you know what a long ride that is? I can't believe you abandoned me like that, Mom." She turns on her heel and storms out.

Right. I'm the one who abandoned her.

I never once remember my father picking me up or driving me anywhere when I was a child. He left when I was eight, and I probably only saw him eight times after that. I never thought Mike would be that kind of father.

On the other hand, I never thought I'd be the kind of mother to lay in bed all day and forget she was supposed to pick her daughter up. My mom was—and still is—habitually late. Whenever I had to stay after for extracurricular activities, I was always the last one at school, waiting for my ride to show. In those days, we didn't have cell phones. I kept a stash of quarters in my bag so I could call her. Most often, she wasn't at home, so I had to hang up after three rings, lest the answering machine pick up and I'd lose my precious twenty-five cents.

I swore I'd never let my kids feel like they didn't matter enough to be on time.

But on the other hand, it didn't seem to matter to them—or to Mike—that I was on time, or early even, every single other time. How many minutes and hours of my own precious time have I spent waiting on them?

My own precious time. That's a laugh. It was never precious to anyone. Not to my mom. Not to my husband. Not to my kids.

And not to me, apparently.

The house phone jangles, forcing me to finally get out of bed. My mom's name on the caller ID makes me wonder if cosmically she knew I was thinking about her.

"I called your cell, and it went right to voicemail."

"Yeah, it's dead. I need to charge it." I dig my phone out from under a blanket and take it over to the charging station on my desk.

"Dead? Is there something wrong with it? I know how you are about battery percentages."

I shrug, though she can't see it. Normally, the thought of a low battery makes me anxious and jittery. However, right now is anything but normal.

"I wasn't feeling well today. I took a nap."

"Do you have another infection? You can't afford to have any more complications. You need to get back out on the dating scene, and no one is going to want to date someone without breasts. Have you scheduled your follow-up surgery yet? When can the implants go back in?"

It's a lot of questions all at once, and I don't have the energy to think about or answer them.

"Mom, I'm not even entertaining the idea of dating. Not now. Not ever. So it doesn't really matter what's going on with my chest."

"What do you mean, not ever? You are only forty-five years old, Margot. You have to put yourself back out there. Sure, the pickings may be slim and beggars can't be choosers, but you need to pull yourself up by the bootstraps and find a new man."

Oh Mom and her metaphors.

Also, Mom and her complete and total inability to be alone.

In the long list of faults my mom has, to me, this was always number one.

Unless I was standing outside in the freezing cold, waiting for her, and then it was number two.

But I never could understand why she went from man to man. Loser to loser. Why she thought she needed to be with someone in order to be her best self, when she should have been focusing on herself first.

I look at the mess around me and that is me. Obviously, I totally have taking care of myself mastered.

She's well intentioned. At least she thinks she is. She wants the best for me, even though she doesn't really know what that is. But she's struck a nerve nonetheless. That nagging thought that I've been trying to push to the deep recesses of my brain, using spoonfuls of ice cream to shove it back there:

Who will want me like this?

Mike, who promised to love me in sickness and in health, didn't want me when my breasts were perfectly reconstructed. He claimed to love them as they were. Dr. Chung had really done a fantastic job in the first go 'round.

Who knows what they'll end up looking like now? Or how long that will take.

Plus healing time.

Best-case scenario, I'm about eight months out from even being able to consider dating. Mentally and emotionally, I'm about eight years.

At the very minimum.

What keeps running through my mind is that I don't know how I could have been better. Done better. I know that if I did, Mike wouldn't have cheated. He wouldn't have left.

In all honesty, I don't know what more I could have done.

CHAPTER 13

"Why don't you put it out on Facebook that you are looking for work? You never know who might know of something."

Becky's logic is sound and probably true.

Of course, there's no way in hell I'm putting it out there for the whole world to see that I'm unemployed and desperate for a job.

I haven't even changed my status yet. I'm not going to be one of those people who advertises every little bump in the road on social media. Not that this is a bump. This is a schism never to again be joined.

With each passing day, I can't believe I dedicated my whole life to this man. How did I never see him for the selfish ass he truly is?

I stare at his text, angry at his words.

It's Wednesday, the only day of the week I look forward to. Even with *Thom* in UnBRCAble, it's still an hour or so that lifts me up. Every other hour of the week feels as if I have lead chains and weights shackled to my ankles.

Yet here Mike is, threatening to ruin my sixty minutes of escape by swinging by to drop off—in person—another set of documents from his lawyer.

His timing is impeccable, as well as carefully planned. He knew I'd be running out the door and wouldn't have the time to argue or beg him.

I wouldn't beg him if he were the last man on Earth, but he probably doesn't realize that.

Still, the large manilla envelope sits on my front seat, taunting me as I drive to UnBRCAble. I've got to find a lawyer. Hopefully a cheap one who is super competent and vicious and will give Mike exactly what he deserves.

Here's the thing, though. Much like posting on Facebook that I'm looking for a job, I can't go around advertising that I need a divorce lawyer because the man I devoted my life to is a prick.

It would be like taking out an ad that I have flappy boob sacks.

I am not one to go spilling that kind of tea, as the kids would say. Mom was always telling the drama of our house to anyone who would listen.

And even those who didn't want to listen.

It always seemed to me that because she put out so much chaos, she attracted it right back.

I don't need that.

I don't want that.

I want a simple, stable, perfect life.

Is that too much to ask?

Erin's waddling in as I get to the door. I'm not being unkind. She's due in a few weeks, I think, and her walk reflects it.

"Let me get the door for you," I say, pulling it open and stepping aside to let her pass. "How are you feeling?"

"Big. Tired. Excited. Scared."

"That about sums motherhood up. I'd say you're on the right track. You're doing great. And this is just the beginning." I smile at her. Pregnancy really agrees with her, even if she doesn't feel that way.

I wish I had taken the time to knit her a baby blanket or something special. That would be assuming that I knew how to knit. Which I don't. I make a mental note to find something special for her little girl.

"Thanks, Marg. I ... I mean, I have a sister and she has two littles, but is it okay if I pick your brain every now and again? My sister barely has any brain cells left. You are so together. I want to be like you when I grow up."

I start to smile, but my face muscles grow tight as I process her words. If she only knew. "Of course. Anything you need."

I mean that, but I'm not sure she'd be asking for advice if she knew what my life was really like. She definitely wouldn't look up to me.

But I *want* to be the person Erin looks up to. Not just Erin. People in general. And up until I saw that text message on Mike's phone, I thought I was that person. Now I'm a sham. A fraud.

If Erin only knew that I couldn't find a job because I don't have the right—read, *any*—

qualifications. I should warn her about that. Delicately, of course. She needs to know that she can't take time off to raise her child.

Because even though it might be the most important thing she will ever do, it will count against her in the long run. It won't matter that she's capable. It will only matter that she hasn't schlepped to an office every day for eighteen years.

The meeting's going on and people are talking, but I'm not listening. Instead, my mind is whirring with all the things I need to do.

Get a job.

Find a lawyer.

Consider selling the house.

Trade in the car.

Get my boobs back.

Put a voodoo hex on Mike so he can never have another erection.

The list is quite daunting.

I look around the group, with our varied histories and stories. Even before Thom joined, we were an eclectic group from all walks of life. Yet everyone seems happy and settled.

Claudia and her partner have been together forever. Tracey's lovers don't last that long, and her search for the next one takes up most of her time. However, she seems to have found her Mr. Right for the time being. Millie has that storybook romance with her British hunk, finding love while recovering from her prophylactic mastectomy.

Even Erin has the fairy tale, deciding to conceive a baby with a co-worker only to discover they were actually in love. Her story belongs in a romantic movie.

Her story ...

"Oh, Erin!" I speak before my brain has a chance to tell my mouth to shut it. "When the baby thing was a business arrangement, you said you had a lawyer draw up a contract, right? Can I get the name of that lawyer? I'm getting inundated with crap from Mike's attorney, and I need to make sure I don't lose my shirt. Because let's face it, with my empty boobs, no one wants to see that."

Apparently, I have lost my mind, making a joke like that in front of Thom. While I often laugh at the jokes the women here make, I'm not clever enough to come up with them myself.

Heat burns my face, a mix of embarrassment and shame. No one seems to notice. Or maybe they think I'm having a hot flash, which could be a possibility as well.

"His name is Paul ... something Italian. I have it at home. I'll message you his number when I look it up. If you don't hear from me, text me. Pregnancy brain has me practically forgetting my own name."

I smile at her, grateful that she doesn't comment on my no doubt beet-red face, nor the candidness about my breasts. "I remember those days. Well, actually I don't, but I remember that I couldn't remember. It's funny—when I went into men ... had my ovaries removed ... my memory got super spotty. But I haven't forgotten anything in a few weeks, so maybe things are leveling off."

Claudia tilts her head. "Marg, may I ask you something?"

No. Nope. No way, no how.

"Sure," I answer, despite myself.

"How are you feeling overall? Since your surgery, I mean. I know the stuff with your husband is not great, but other than that."

"You mean, 'Other than that, Mrs. Lincoln, how was the play?'" I'm on fire tonight. I should get my own stand-up spot. I'll be here all week. Please tip your waitress.

Her question makes me think though. "Fine, I guess. Actually, now that you mention it, I haven't had a headache since the surgery. And I'm not forgetting things either."

"How about joint pain or intestinal issues?"

Okay, I am *not* talking about my frequent diarrhea in public. Though, now that she mentions it, I've been quite regular since the surgery. "Why?"

"I know even though you're going through a rough patch at home, since your surgery, you seem better. Healthier. Your color is better. I'm wondering if you had BII."

"What's BII?" Thom interrupts.

I roll my eyes. "Breast implant illness. It's where your body makes you sick from the implants."

He nods. "So are you better? Maybe you shouldn't get implants if they make you sick."

My eye roll turns into a glare. "I'm pretty sure that's none of your business."

"Just stating the obvious here. I agree with Claudia. You do look different. Maybe you shouldn't go back to implants."

I am now officially pushed over my breaking point.

I jump to my feet. "And maybe—*just maybe*—you should not comment on things that have nothing to do with your body. Or about body parts that you do not possess. You have no idea what it's like to have multiple parts ripped out of your body. To lose all the hormones that give you youth, vitality, and a sex drive. To have to go the extra mile to feel like a woman because all of your femininity was cut out with a scalpel. You don't have anyone telling you to lop off your balls and then broadcast it every day that you don't have nuts. Though knowing you, you probably would."

Without another word, I storm out.

Once I'm safe in my car I realize that I just had a full-on Karen meltdown in the middle of UnBRCAble.

I can never go back there again.

On the other hand, I will never have to see Thom again either, which is something I can totally live with.

CHAPTER 14

I am an idiot.

Desperation does that to a person, and I've reached new highs—er, lows—with this desperation. I should have paid closer attention to the job I applied for.

I didn't, and now I'm here, in Satan's den.

Otherwise known as the radio station where Thom works. The job seemed harmless enough. Promotions assistant for Liberty Media Corp.

Frankly, I thought it was either a newspaper or an insurance company. A radio station never crossed my mind.

But here I am, in the waiting room with a gigantic photo of TJ the DJ staring at me. Even though it's in black and white, his Hawaiian shirt is still loud enough to hurt my eyes.

Maybe the ugly shirts are part of his persona and he's contractually obligated to wear them. It would be a slightly redeeming quality if he secretly had a closet full of button-down oxfords that he looked at longingly every morning before getting dressed.

But in reality, more than I hope his closet has a secret stash of respectable clothes, I hope that he doesn't see me here. I check my watch. He should be on air right now, so as long as I get in and out, it should be fine. I think I would die if Thom saw me here, interviewing for a job I can't get and frankly have no business even applying for.

They tend not to look highly on people who don't have any idea what the company does or what the position entails.

"Margot Kensington? I'm Jack Smalls, Director of WBRC."

I stand to meet the man, quickly taking in the fact that he's wearing jeans and a faded Rolling Stones T-shirt. I get (now) that this is a radio station, but is this really how one dresses to meet interviewees? Suddenly, I feel ridiculous in my pencil skirt, buttoned-up blouse, and blazer. I'm wearing sensible pumps and panty hose, for Christ's sake, and this guy is wearing Birkenstocks with socks in the middle of February. I am obviously in the wrong place at the wrong time looking for the wrong thing.

I stand up, shaking his hand and following him into his office. I don't know why I'm even bothering. This will just be another rejection. Another time I'm trying hard, following all the rules, and it's not enough.

Screw this.

Jack Smalls starts his spiel, and I do my best not to tune him out. It doesn't matter what the needs of this position are. It doesn't matter that I could probably do it in my sleep with one hand tied behind my back. All that will matter to Jack Smalls are the empty years on my resume.

"So, tell me, Margot, what qualifies you for this position?"

I cringe at the use of my full name. It sounds so foreign to my ears. Sure, I'd tried using it, making the transition when I started high school. It seemed perfect to me. I was more mature and would use a more mature name.

If only it hadn't rhymed with another word for prostitute.

Kids can be cruel.

And it seems that some of them never grow out of it.

"Well, as you can see, Jack, I don't have tons of experience in the work field per se."

"Tons of experience? You don't actually have any in this field."

It's not untrue, but I feel foolish enough already. His words sting like hand sanitizer on a paper cut.

Yet suddenly, I don't care. I have nothing left to lose.

"Yes, true. Let's be honest, until I walked through the doors, I had no idea what Liberty Media Group was. I was thinking it was insurance. But my husband is a cheating louse, and I'm pretty sure he's about to hang me out to dry, leaving me destitute. Even though my nickname in high school, thanks to some evil, jealous bitches was 'Margot the Ho,' I'm too old to work the corner, so that's not an option either. No office will even consider hiring me because I've only worked a handful of hours per week while I was raising my kids. They won't let me show them how I can organize and streamline and make things run better."

I sit back in the chair, a little stunned by the explosion of verbal diarrhea. I'm sure when it sinks in, I will be mortified and horrified at what I said, but in this very moment, I feel relieved.

It felt so good to get that all off my chest.

Jack Smalls tents his fingers under his chin like an evil mastermind. I'm sure he's at a loss for words. I know I now am.

"Interesting."

I open my mouth but then close it quickly again when I realize there really is nothing more to say.

"Here at Liberty Media, we're big believers in soft skills. Let's face it, this is radio. Either you have that *je ne sais quois* or you don't. It's not something easily quantified on a resume, which is why we rely so heavily on our interviews."

Well crap.

Kind of wish he'd led with that.

Go figure—the one job I could have had if I'd stayed cool, calm, and collected, I blew with my mouth and my rage and my story of Margot the Ho.

I stand up. "I'll see myself out."

Jack Smalls stands too. "Wait a minute, Margot."

I can't take it any longer. "Marg, with a hard g at the end. Just Marg. Please." I add the last word on so I don't sound as harsh.

"Okay, Marg with a hard g. Before you go, tell me about your organizational skills. You are without a doubt the most put together person we've had apply here in a while. We are looking for someone who has their shit together."

"May I offer a suggestion?"

Jack Smalls sits back down and gestures for me to do the same. Tentatively I perch on the edge of the chair, my posture impeccable. If I had breasts, they'd have been sticking straight out.

"Don't conduct interviews looking like you just woke up from an all-night rager. Don't say words like 'shit' while you're interviewing. If you hold yourself to higher standards, the world around you will follow suit."

He blinks slowly. Once. Twice. Then, he bursts out laughing. "Marg, that's great. Perfect. You're hired."

Now it's my turn to do the slow blink. "Huh?"

"You are what we need around here. You are straight-talking and aren't afraid to lay it all out there for the world to see."

I think he has me mistaken for someone who lays it all out there for the world to see. I don't want anyone to ever see what a disaster I am. I don't talk about it in public. I don't advertise it on social media. And I certainly don't bring it to work.

I need to bring this interview around before Jack Smalls thinks I'm something that I'm not. "So tell me, what exactly would this job entail? Specifically."

I like specifics. I like details. I can do my best—be my best—when I'm well prepared.

"You know, the usual. Setting up and organizing promotions. Scheduling talent. Making sure everything's ready to go and the talent is where they need to be."

Talent. I get a little chill thinking about that. I would be responsible for booking talent. Like actual celebrities. Famous people. Rock stars.

"Okay, sounds great. I'll take it."

I may have lost my mind. Before I know it, I've filled out a stack of paperwork and have agreed to start tomorrow. Well, actually, it's three hours later, and I've had to text Bailey to tell her to take the bus home from school.

That, of course, makes me feel guilty, but I don't see what else I can do. I'm sure there's a way to balance being a working woman and the perfect mother. Lots of women have done it. I simply need to figure out their secrets.

At least I have a job.

Sure, the pay isn't great, and I might have to work the occasional weekend. There's the chance that I might run into Thom, but if he's on the air, I'll be in the office, and I won't have to see him. He's probably out of here before I really even get started for the day. Still, it's a job and they want me.

I think that last part is the most attractive thing. They wanted *me*. Jack Smalls didn't care that I've been out of the full-time hustle. He believes in me to do this job. He could see that I am organized and detail-oriented and efficient.

With how long it took them to get the paperwork together for me to fill out, it's not hard to see how much they need me here. Buoyed by this hope, on my way out the door, I pull up the number for the lawyer Erin sent me.

It's time to get moving on my new life. I'm gonna cut Mike out like I did with the cancer. My breast tumor was small—less than a centimeter. Mike is two hundred pounds that is killing me. I'm going to excise him and start brand new.

This time, I'm going to get it right. Everything will be perfect from now on.

CHAPTER 15

The list that should be entitled, "Reasons why I'm an idiot," is growing longer by the minute. Number one on that list has to be telling Mike that I got a job. It was probably because when I called him, his response was, "Oh wait, let me guess—you need more money."

Truth was, I was sharing the news with him because it was my instinct to do that. He's been my go-to person for twenty years. He's been regularly texting me about dumbass crap, like what is *his* grandmother's last name. I should go in and change all the answers to his security questions just to mess with him.

But today, I dialed him without even thinking. I was so thrown by his tone that I sputtered out, "No. I just got a job, so I should be set."

The a-hole laughed—*laughed*—at me. His response, "Who did you find that's going to pay you to nag them?"

His cruelty stunned me into silence, so I disconnected without saying a word.

I should have called Becky.

The second item on my list would be showing up to the aforementioned new job in professional business attire. I should have realized from my interview that this is a casual place. It's been a while since I've been a nine-to-fiver, but I wasn't raised to go to work in ripped jeans. Or sneakers. Or ugly Hawaiian shirts.

Dressing is a nightmare right now. Most of my old wardrobe doesn't work anymore. I used to have D-cups. With my sacks of skin, I'm probably about an A, maybe a B if I fold them up in a creative way. With the encouragement from the UnBRCAble ladies, I ordered a pair of pillow prostheses for the interim.

Yes, they are exactly what you are thinking. I'm forty-five years old and back to stuffing my bra.

But every time I try to use them, I'm so terrified that one will ride up or slip out or something equally as mortifying that I haven't worked up the nerve to wear them outside the house.

And I don't want to spend the money on the specialized clothing meant to hold them in place. It's highway robbery.

Thus, the limitations in my clothing vex me as I try to get dressed. Nothing clingy. Nothing low cut. Nothing that doesn't button up to my chin. But then there are the hot flashes, so I need full coverage that is also light and breathable.

I settle on a chiffon royal blue high-necked blouse from Ann Taylor with smart, trim black pants and high-heeled black boots. I wasn't sure what the heat would be like (for when I'm not hot flashing), so I add a black blazer. Definitely more business casual than the suit I wore the other day, but not casual enough.

Not only do I look out of place, but I feel it too when Thom walks by and says, "What's up, Senator? Are you scheduled for negotiations with the United Nations after this?"

"I'm a professional. You should try acting like one sometime," I retort before I can stop myself.

Which brings me to reason three of why I'm an idiot.

It never occurred to me that the "talent" at a radio station refers to the on-air employees. You know, the disc jockeys.

That's right. TJ the DJ.

TJ and Todd are the biggest names at the station and therefore the most sought-after talents. Additionally, because of their morning drive shift, they are prime candidates for doing afternoon and early evening appearances.

I won't be working with rock stars; I'll be working with Thom.

Make that working *for* Thom.

Though Jack had pitched the position as the person to organize and run things, in reality, I'm an overgrown gopher and babysitter. Except I'm at his beck and call.

It's my job to make sure Thom's on time and looks presentable (HA!), and the company car has gas, and he has his beverage of choice. I have to tell him where he's supposed to be when and what prizes and businesses he's promoting.

I'm his bitch.

Thom looks at my feet and then back up at me. "You have no idea what you're doing here, do you?"

"It's my first day on the job. I have a lot to learn." I fold my arms defiantly over my chest.

"Lesson number one: wear comfortable shoes."

"I'm fine."

Thom looks down at my feet again. "You won't be. Trust me. Comfortable shoes, Marg." He emphasizes the g so hard that he adds an extra sound, making it sound like he's saying Marg-a. He turns to walk away.

Oh no, I can't let him leave like that.

"Whatever you say, Thom."

He turns back, stepping in so close we're practically nose to nose. "TJ. Never anything but TJ here. Got it?"

The serious tone to his voice catches me off guard. I swallow hard and nod.

The intensity in his light brown eyes is too much for me to handle, so I look down and mumble an apology. Instead of turning away in a huff or berating me, he leans in, his perpetual five o'clock shadow brushing my cheek, and whispers in my ear, "I know you understand what it's like to have a thing about names."

And then he's gone.

My legs feel a bit weak, and all the confidence I had whooshes out of me. Thom—er, TJ—is a joker and a clown. He's sardonic and satirical. He's quick to poke fun at others, so I didn't expect this serious side of him.

It's enough to make me doubt, even more so, the decision to take this job. For the remainder of the morning, I keep my head down, trying to make sense of emails and arrangements. There are documents and scraps of paper all over the place.

I don't know how anyone ever showed up on time, let alone showed up at all. Jack Smalls has given me little direction on what I'm supposed to do this morning, so I do the thing I'm good at.

Organizing. Planning. Making sense out of nonsense.

Hours later, I have a color-coded spreadsheet linked to a calendar and task list that I share with Jack. Two minutes later, he comes sprinting out to my desk.

"What is this?" he pants, pointing at my computer screen. "Wha ... what have you been doing?"

I look at the screen and the time catches my eye. Crap. I've been at this all day. "Sorry. I didn't mean for it to take so long. It was hard with only one screen. For my bookkeeping work, I'm used to two screens, so it makes it go faster."

"But what *is* this?" he asks again.

"A spreadsheet? Calendar? Task list? I wasn't sure whose responsibility most of the tasks are, so I color coded them but didn't officially assign them. I don't want to miss something I'm supposed to do."

Jack's mouth hangs open as he looks from me to my computer screen. Finally, he shakes his head.

"Fine. Tomorrow, you're inventorying the swag room." As he starts to walk away, he turns back, waving his hand in my direction "You won't want to look like *that*."

CHAPTER 16

"Mrs. Kensington, I'm so glad to reach you finally."

I turn my phone off for one hour to meet with the lawyer, and *this* is what happens.

It's never a good sign when the principal of the school is calling you.

Never.

"Yes, Mr. Levin? What can I help you with?" My voice is high and tight, and I'm fairly certain my blood pressure has just doubled.

"There was an incident with Jordan today. In the locker room following PE class."

My blood pressure has officially tripled.

Oh God, what could have happened? "Is he okay?"

"Actually, no. He was injured in an altercation. The school nurse thinks he should probably have his hand looked at. She would have called you herself, but I told her I needed to speak to you."

"Altercation? Hurt?" My mind is whizzing a million miles an hour as I apply my foot to the gas and take the turn onto Sherman Street a bit faster than I should.

I'm appreciative for the horsepower of the Cayenne. Who knows how fast I'll be able to drive when I trade it in for a low-end (and lower cost) vehicle? "What happened? How did he get hurt?"

"Apparently, Jordan was injured during a fight with another student. The nurse thinks he may have broken a bone in his hand. You should probably consider getting it x-rayed."

"But it's swim season! He has sectionals next week."

"Perhaps he should have thought of that before throwing blows. Due to our zero-tolerance policy, Jordan will be suspended."

Suspended? No, it can't be. The blood pounds in my head so hard I worry something may rupture. Suspensions happen to hoodlums and kids from no-good families.

Kids like my brother.

Not my child.

Except it is.

What are people going to say? Mike is going to blow a gasket. He's going to say this is my fault. He might even try to take the kids from me. I need to do damage control, and I need to do it *now*.

"Mr. Levin, I agree that this sort of behavior cannot be tolerated, and that punishment is indeed warranted. However, knowing Jordan as I do, I question that an out-of-school suspension is the best answer for him. He may view it as a vacation and not think about his actions. He might be better served with an in-school suspension. This way, he'll be forced to confront the repercussions of his actions."

The silence on the line has me questioning if I've pressed my luck on this. Mr. Levin's mercurial moods are legendary, so it's impossible to tell if I'm catching him on the upswing or downswing.

"That's an interesting point, Mrs. Kensington."

Interesting good? Interesting bad? Interesting yes and then no one will know Jordan was suspended because he's still in school?

"Can you bring Jordan in on Monday? We'll have a brief meeting where we discuss and agree on the terms of his in-school, and you both will sign off on it. If there is any breach, Jordan will be suspended, out of school, no questions asked."

Monday. I'm supposed to meet with Jack on my two-week review. I fully anticipate being fired. It took me six days to clean out and organize the swag room. Every time Jack walked by, he shook his head in disapproval.

That meeting is at nine.

"Certainly. We will be there at seven-twenty." Should give me enough time to get to work by eight so I can pack my things before I get fired. I cross my fingers and silently pray that Mr. Levin agrees on the time.

"Thank you for your support, Mrs. Kensington. I'm sorry to see Jordan making such poor choices. You can pick him up now."

His words cut through me like a sharp blade, as if I'm the one making poor choices. It doesn't matter that

KATHRYN R. BIEL

it's Jordan, not me. My child is an extension of me, so I might as well have been the one throwing the punch.

Instead, I feel as though I'm on the receiving end of a closed fist. It's only February, and this year can suck it.

I don't even want to ask what else can happen, because I know fate will laugh her ass off while showing me.

Instead, I focus on breathing and meditation. It's the only way I can think of to prevent myself from going postal on Jordan as he approaches the car, escorted by a security guard.

My son, being escorted by a man in uniform, like he is a common criminal. I want to die of embarrassment and beat him into the ground all at the same time. How could he do this to me? Doesn't he know what this looks like?

He gets in the car, as sullen as ever. Instead of peppering him with questions, I grip the steering wheel tightly. This incident is the last thing I need right now.

I look straight ahead, not even blinking. I can feel Jordan staring at me. I don't know if he's waiting for me to yell at him or oh-poor-baby him.

Option one finally wins.

"What were you thinking? No, you know what? Don't answer that. I don't want to know because there is nothing you can tell me that will make this right. That can fix this situation. That can erase this from your record or make your hand unbroken or get you back on the swim team before sectionals. Nothing. You screwed this up."

"Jesus, Mom, you don't think I know that? But thanks for the support. I really appreciate your belief in me."

His words are like knives to my already torn-up heart. I wish I could pull over and take him into my arms like I did when he was a toddler with a skinned knee.

But he's practically an adult and needs to take responsibility for his actions.

"Don't get mad at me. I'm not the one who punched ..." I trail off. I have no idea who he even got into a fight with. Or why. Maybe I do need to hear his side of the story. Perhaps he was defending his sister or a classmate that someone was picking on.

Yes, that's what it has to be. My boy, standing up for those who don't have a voice.

"Tabor Tyner."

"Tabor? From Quaker Road?"

"Do you know of any other losers named Tabor?" he sneers.

"No, I don't. Why were you fighting?"

"I can't stand that kid. He's annoying."

I wait for Jordan to say more, but he doesn't. The sound of the turn signal fills the car, marking the beats of silence like a metronome.

"That's it. He's annoying."

"He's been annoying the piss out of me since kindergarten. I couldn't deal with his crap anymore."

That's it. His crap. Which, with the attitude Jordan is presenting, is probably nothing.

Jordan is turning into Mike with each passing moment. This is a fact that I hadn't seen coming. I mean, sure, he looks just like his father. He's smart and handsome.

But he's also demanding and ... toxic.

The word pops into my head before I can stop it.

It's the perfect descriptor of my soon-to-be ex.

I can't let my son turn into him.

"Jordan, you know better than this. I'm not sure what this 'crap' is because you haven't articulated anything. Instead, you resorted to violence, which is never the answer. Never." I pull into the parking lot of the ortho urgent care. "Do you understand me?"

Jordan opens his car door, slamming it shut behind him. "All I understand is that I'll never be the perfect son you want me to be. I don't know why I even bother. I can't live up to your expectations. Maybe I should stop even trying."

I follow him out. "You mean like your father did?"

"Maybe he had the right idea. Getting away from you is the only smart thing to do."

His words are a slap to my face. Any small bit of composure I've been grasping onto slips away. "Okay, fine. Call your father. He can take care of this. I hope the hand doesn't hurt too much, since you can't be seen without parental consent. You'll have to wait until he gets here. If he gets here. I believe he has weekend ... plans ... with Emily."

And I get back in the car and drive away.

Okay, I drive around the block and circle back so I can watch Jordan to make sure he's okay. I'm mad, but I haven't lost all my mothering instincts. Also, I'm about seventy-five percent sure Mike won't take

Jordan's call to begin with, and even if he does, he won't come here.

Mike can't handle parenting. I've been the default parent since day one. Even when the kids were little, even when I was recovering from my mastectomy and reconstruction, I was the default parent. You know, the one responsible for all the things. For making all the decisions and planning the logistics and carrying the mental load.

Mike never saw the load that I carried, but never felt shy about questioning my decisions either.

Totally toxic.

I don't know how I didn't see it before.

Words from my grandmother float through my head. "It's better to be slapped with the truth than kissed by a lie."

My whole life has been a lie. A sham. A farce.

I see Jordan, sitting on the curb. He puts his phone to his ear and his mouth moves for a few seconds before disconnecting. He had to leave a voicemail.

Mike is a slime.

But his son needs to learn his lesson, so I wait. Five minutes. Then ten. Jordan picks up his phone again. Still no answer.

I can see his heart breaking as the realization dawns on him. In turn, my heart breaks for my baby boy, alone and in pain. Obviously hurt and angry as well.

I practically floor it as I pull back into the parking lot. If it was a movie or TV show, the brakes would squeal as the car swerved to a stop right in front of Jordan. However, it's irresponsible to drive like that, so I park in an available slot and walk up to my son, trying to hold my shoulders square and my head high so that he won't see that I'm as gutted as he is.

"Come on, let's go see about that hand."

Jordan looks up at me, his eyes shining. "He didn't answer. He didn't call back."

"I know, honey."

I want to tell him, but moreover I want him to see that I'm here for him. That he and his sister are the most important things in the world to me, and that they are why I've tried so hard.

Maybe too hard.

CHAPTER 17

"Slumming it today, Madam Secretary?" Thom says as I ditch my coat on the back of my chair. I've just come from the meeting with Mr. Levin and have about an hour before my boss tells me how utterly incompetent and disappointing I am. I am having yet another banner day. With the weekend I had, it was all I could do to take a shower and get out of my pajamas. Washing my hair this morning wasn't a priority, though I didn't realize it was that obvious. My jeans are a dark wash and look like formal wear compared to what others here routinely don.

"Shouldn't you be in the booth?"

"We're on our commercial break, so I came to get some coffee, since the PA didn't answer her phone." He looks pointedly at the phone on my desk.

Yes, that's right. I get to fetch coffee for Thom when he's on the air. None of the other DJs ask me to get them their coffee, but I think Thom takes a secret sadistic pleasure in making me serve him.

Actually, there's nothing secret about it.

"You know I delight in having you fetch my coffee. You're so good at it. Efficient too. Perfect, really." He continues, his tone so mocking that I want to punch him.

Maybe I should be more understanding with Jordan. Who is serving one day of in-school suspension, only has a bruised hand, and can return to swimming practice on Wednesday, thank you very much.

Not that anyone appreciates my efforts, least of all Jordan.

"I had a meeting this morning for my son, not that it matters to you. And then I have to meet with Jack. After that, I'm supposed to be cleaning out the back room. How many rooms of crap are there in here to begin with?"

Thom holds up his coffee. "I shall never tell. Gotta run."

Ten minutes later, Jack emails me that he's canceling the meeting and to work in the back room. Okay.

At least I'm not being fired today.

But after an hour in the back room, I sort of wish I was. This is the room where old swag and garbage go to breed and spawn and create more crap than an episode of *Hoarders*.

It's clear to see that I'm being punished. Either that or Jack is trying to make this so difficult that I quit and then they won't have to pay unemployment for me.

Little does he know that I need this job, and I'm too stubborn to quit.

A few hours later, I stumble out into the hall, desperate for natural light and fresh air. I've created a few paths in the room and begun sorting. I can see this cleanup may take another several days.

In some ways, it's good because then I don't have to work with Thom at all. I dread the time when we have to go out and do an event together. I much prefer the organization behind the scenes.

Not to mention, Thom is so unpredictable that who knows what he might say about me in front of people. He knows much more than I'm comfortable with him knowing. I don't trust him not to call me out on things while he's performing for a crowd.

I hate being in a place where I don't feel secure. It's how I spent my entire childhood, and I thought I'd moved past that. I thought I'd built a life of stability and security.

I thought wrong, obviously.

I head back to my workstation to get a drink of water and email Jack some suggestions, including donating swag with outdated logos or personalities to charity for use since we can no longer give it away as promotional material.

Jack responds with an email telling me to do whatever I want and that I should plan on working the Women's Expo with TJ and Todd this weekend. I can take a day off in compensation or get overtime.

Overtime is a perk I didn't count on.

On the other hand, Jordan has sectionals on Saturday, so I quickly email Jack back that I am unavailable that day but will be happy to work overtime on Sunday.

It's a lie, of course, because I don't want to give up my Sunday. I don't want to be at Thom's beck and call and be his gopher. I'd be much happier making schedules and taking inventory and lining up events than actually being at them. But since this was the job I was hired for, I can't complain. I can't let the team down, even if Thom is a part of it.

~~~**~~~

"No, absolutely not."

He has got to be kidding me. Really.

I look at the wisp of a tank top Thom is holding out to me. It's barely 8:00 a.m., and he wants me to slip into something a whole lot more uncomfortable.

"Come on, Marg. All the employees wear them. Sarah's got hers on."

Sarah is also twenty-two and probably a triple D. Even when I had breasts, they never filled out a tank top like that.

"You don't," I quickly retort.

Of course, he's wearing another Hawaiian shirt. I'm starting to wonder how many he has. I don't know that I've ever seen the same one twice.

"I'm not an employee. I'm the talent. Not to mention, it gets really warm and stuffy in here as the place fills with people. You'll thank me for the tank top. I sweated my ass off yesterday. Now go change. You have to."

I wore cropped, fitted jeans. I wore my cute little low-top Converse sneakers (with memory foam insoles because I'm not as young as I used to be). I also wore a baggy sweater over a baggy shirt because ... boobs.

Or lack thereof.

There is no way in hell I can wear a shirt like that. I probably can't wear any of the station's ladies' apparel, with their fitted form and scoop necks.

I cock my head to the side. "I can't wear that. I *won't* wear that. Nowhere in the stuff from human resources does it say I have to. No."

"How are people going to know who you are here representing? We need the station name everywhere, including right across your chest."

Fire fills my cheeks, and my eyes sting as I will myself not to cry.

Just when I think I'm starting to pick up the pieces of my crumbled life, my breast cancer crap has to come roaring back in.

I'd assure myself with the fact that he doesn't know what he's saying, except that he does. He knows the truth about me and what I'm concealing with layers of shapeless clothing, no matter how hot it makes me.

I shift my gaze to the floor as my tears refuse to obey my commands for them to evaporate.

"TJ," I lean in and whisper, "*Thom*, you know why I can't wear that shirt. Why I can't advertise for the station on my chest." I work up the courage to look at him.

His brow furrows as he cocks his head. "Marg, I don't know what you're talking about. You wear brand names all the time. It's not above your moral code. I understand that you normally like to be all fancy and formal, but this is what the appropriate dress code is for this event."

GAH!

How can one man be so obtuse?

I grab him by the arm and pull him around to behind where our booth is set up. There's a background din that won't let me whisper my words, but this is certainly not something I want to broadcast.

He starts talking before I can find the words.

"I get that this is not your usual style, but it's the uniform. It's bright orange and turquoise so you get noticed. You need to deal with it."

"Thom, I cannot wear that shirt. I'm between surgeries," I hiss.

He looks at me, blinking slowly.

I continue. "You know that. I'm waiting for reconstruction. I can't advertise on my chest because I haven't got one currently."

His gaze drops for a nanosecond and then quickly returns to my eyes. Then, without warning, his arms are around me, and he pulls me in close. I feel my virtually flat breast area squash into him.

He's probably only an inch taller than me, so my chin slides naturally onto his shoulder. "Marg, I forgot. I ... well, I don't really spend my day thinking about your breasts, and it never occurred to me. I'm sorry. I thought it was because the shirt was too ugly for you. I know how you hate bright colors."

I pull back a little, though still in his arms. "How could you forget? I mean, there's nothing there."

His hold loosens, and I step back. "Believe it or not, I don't spend all my time looking at my colleagues' assets. If I did, I wouldn't be looking at you."

Ouch.

He continues. "I mean, I'm much more of an ass man, and have you seen what a fine ass Todd has?"

For the record, Todd does not have a fine ass, and for once, I can see the humor that makes TJ the DJ so captivating.

I look down at my feet. Since it seems we're having a moment of honesty, I say what's on my mind. "I thought you were doing it on purpose because you don't like me. Like you were trying to get me to quit."

"Quit?"

"Yeah, so that the station doesn't have to pay unemployment. Jack doesn't like me; you don't like me."

"Why do you say that?"

"TJ, where you at?" a voice bellows. It's Todd, the deep timbre unmistakable. "We're on in two."

Thom looks at me for a beat, and then he's gone.

What is it about him that brings out the worst in me? It's like I lose my filter and my awareness of everything. I can't believe I told him I thought they were trying to force me out.

Never admit your weaknesses. Never let them see the chink in your armor. When they see it, they exploit it. It gives them the perfect target to aim for.

I need you. I can't live without you.

I can hear my mother saying those words to my father—and then to countless flavors of the month. As soon as she said them, it was the beginning of the end.

I wait a minute, and then two, before I walk around to the front of the booth. I stare ahead into the crowd, willing my brain not to glance at Thom. He knows so much about me. He's seen me at my worst.

I'm not sure I was ever this vulnerable in front of Mike, and he still left me.

Not that it's the same, because it's not like there's a relationship between Thom and I, nor will there ever be. I see him more as an enemy, and if my closest confidant rejected me, what would my nemesis do with such an easy target?

Suddenly, something soft *whops* me upside the head. My hands go up to shield my face and come down in a tangle of orange fabric. I work to unscramble the pile and find a men's XL T-shirt.

I look over at Thom, and he dips his chin ever so slightly. Without saying a word, I head to the bathroom to change. This shirt swims on my frame and looks ridiculous.

But at least my boob sacks aren't exposed.

Being a child of the 80s, when oversized, neon clothes were the style, I know just what to do. I quickly roll the sleeves and use a hair tie to cinch the shirt in on my hip. This creates a nice blousy effect, which takes the emphasis off my chest area.

Maybe it even looks cute with my slim jeans and Converse.

I turn in the mirror.

Not cute, but about as good as I'm going to get right now.

As I head back out into the din of the Expo, it occurs to me that this was a very nice thing Thom did for me.

He didn't have to, and let's face it, I probably don't deserve it. Maybe he doesn't hate me.

A year ago, I would have had a spring in my step and a smile on my face as I returned to work, buoyed by the thought that hard work and competence has won me favor.

Instead, I'm now suspicious that he's trying to make me relax and feel good so it stings that much more when the rug is pulled out. Call me paranoid all you want. I wasn't paranoid at all in my marriage and look how that turned out. I was so naive it is laughable.

Mike bought a dress in her size, not mine. I took it as a weight-loss goal.

He claimed to be working to cover for nonabsent co-workers. I assumed he was buying me gifts.

He was in contact with a realtor. I assumed he was pursuing our lifelong dreams.

I was a fool.

I will not be again.

I have to watch my back around Thom.

CHAPTER 18

"I've lost three more pounds."

Becky sighs. "Marg, you don't need to be losing any more weight. You're so thin now that if you turned sideways, you could hide behind a blade of grass."

"I know. I'm not trying. I'm supposed to be gaining weight right now."

"You? Gain weight? Says who?" She laughs. I can hear her eye roll over the phone.

"Dr. Chung. He's worried that I won't have enough spare fat to harvest to make new breasts out of."

I'm supposed to put on at least five pounds. Well, more like ten. Instead, I'm now negative fifteen. And this is without the grapefruit and coffee diet.

Stress, man.

I've now learned that with minor to moderate stress levels, I eat my feelings. With massive stress, my appetite packs up and leaves, and then my ulcer handles the rest.

So much fun.

"Yeah, well, look on the bright side. At least you will be bikini ready without trying this year."

Her words, though well intentioned, sting. It's hard to wear a bikini—or any bathing suit for that matter—without breasts. And to be perfectly honest, relaxing on the beach is the furthest thing from my mind.

I'm three months out from my last surgery, which technically puts me in the zone to start reconstruction again. The reality is that even if I wasn't shedding pounds like a cat sheds fur, I really can't consider surgery right now.

I don't have that kind of sick time, and I need the paycheck. Mike is paying child support, but the car's lease and the mortgage is killing me.

The Porsche is going next week. The lease on the Kia will be more manageable. Still, I probably need to sell the house and downsize into something more reasonable.

Of course, that's the last thing I want to do because of the kids. It will be so hard on them, and they don't need any more trauma right now.

And I need to do that first before I can convalesce for three months. The DIEP flap reconstruction recovery can be brutal. It's at least twelve hours on the operating table, if that tells you anything. It will take lots of careful coordination of schedules, and I'll need to ask my mom to come stay with me.

If she will.

Otherwise, without that help, there's probably no way it will work.

"Maybe next year. Best-case scenario, if I can gain the weight, I'll have to wait until summer when the kids are out of school anyway."

"Oh, hey! I have an idea! Can you see about having donor fat cells for your new boobs? I've got enough to spare to make Dolly Parton jealous."

I laugh at Becky's offer. "I'm pretty sure they don't do that, but I'll ask."

Becky has been my sanity these past three months. Even though we don't see each other much, she's a voice of reason and understanding.

Also, she offered to slice off Mike's junk. Any friend who will cut someone on your behalf is a friend worth having.

"Well, if I can manage to get approved for surgery, it'll all depend on whether my mom can come out here for a while to help."

"Oh crap, man. I'm sorry."

While normally I appreciate Becky's bluntness, it's not what I want to hear today. "I know." I sigh. "Any chance you want to adopt me for a few months? I promise I'll be good."

I'm right back to feeling how I did when I was a kid, when my dad first left. I remember swearing that oath to him—and meaning it with every fiber of my being—if only he'd come back.

And just like it did almost forty years ago, the deal is not agreed upon. "You know I can't. This is the summer we are doing the cross-country thing."

Becky and her husband have been saving for years to buy an RV and take the entire summer off, communing with nature and all that crap. I hadn't been jealous when she first told me about her plans, but the idea of her having a husband with which to plan such an adventure makes me sad. I mean, not sad that Becky is going but sad that I no longer have the family dynamic that would make this possible. I'd thought Mike and I would take the kids to Europe someday soon, before Jordan goes to college.

I'd better start playing the lottery if I ever want to make that happen now.

"I can't believe you won't give up your dreams and lifelong plans to take care of me. How rude," I say lightly, hoping my tone masks the sadness welling up within.

That sadness stays with me as I walk into UnBRCAble a few hours later. When it comes around to me, I share the bind I find myself in. "Does anyone want to adopt my kids and me for the summer? You can live in my house, assuming I have one by then. It'll be lots of fun, driving me around and helping me wipe."

"Are you telling me you don't have a bidet yet?" Millie interjects. "Seriously, it's life changing. I will never go back to plain toilet paper again."

In many other circles, this conversation would be awkward and inappropriate. Here, it's our reality.

Thom, to his credit, just sits there with his stupid lollipop stick in his mouth, not saying anything. He's been doing better, not questioning the things we say.

It makes me hate him a little less.

And frankly, I'm so desperate for some help that I let my guard down in front of him. I pretend that Thom and TJ the DJ are two totally different people. It's stupid, I know, but it's the only way I can still get what I need out of this group and face him at work.

"I have the bidet, of course. I was being dramatic. The benefit is that no one will have to help me through my period," I add glibly.

Okay, I did *not* mean to say that in front of Thom. My cheeks burn in embarrassment.

The other women laugh, mostly because we're all in the same surgically induced menopausal boat.

Not having monthly cramps is the *only* benefit of the hysterectomy, as far as I can tell.

"What about your mom? Don't you still have one?" Tracey asks. I am one of the fortunate ones who has not lost her mother to cancer. Frankly, if I hadn't had that suspicious lump—which turned out to be cancer—I don't know that I would ever have been tested for the BRCA mutation.

"Yes, but I'm not sure she's available."

More like willing.

But some things are too private to share, no matter how good the group.

"She came before, right? When you had the implants removed?" Claudia asks.

"Yes, but she couldn't stay long. She has other things to tend to." And by things, I mean her man of the month. If she's between men, she might come and stay. Now how to orchestrate a breakup at exactly the right moment?

I shake the thought out of my head. Living with my mother is like being on a soap opera, and I find myself acting like that when I'm around her. It's not how I want to be, so the distance is usually a good thing.

The subject changes, and I relax back into the couch. Nothing's been resolved. Nothing's changed, yet somehow I feel a little better. It's like the positive energy of this group helped to refill me somehow.

That is, of course, until I'm leaving and Thom stops me, taking my elbow to halt my progress.

"Can I talk to you for a second?"

"No, I don't think so."

His grip tightens slightly, just enough to get my attention. I sigh. "What about, Thom?"

"Work stuff."

Ugh. I don't want to do this. I want to go home and crawl into comfy, yet cool pajamas and sleep until this part of my life is over.

He looks around. "Let's go grab a drink and talk."

This is not high on my list of things I want to do right now. In fact, getting my bikini line waxed and doing an IRS tax audit might rank higher. Speaking of which, I need to have the lawyer figure out how we're filing taxes. Considering Mike left me on December twenty-eighth, I would think we have to file jointly.

Taxes are my jam normally, but divorce makes everything more complicated.

"I can only stay for a little bit. I have to make sure homework is done and my children have not starved to death in my absence." There's actually little chance of that since Jordan eats me out of house and home. It's no wonder I'm losing weight—I can't afford to feed all of us.

"Why don't the kids go with their father on Wednesdays, since you know you'll be out?"

I stop in my tracks, halfway across the parking lot.

Thom keeps walking for a few steps and then turns to look at me. "What?"

"I can't believe I didn't think of that sooner. It's a brilliant idea."

He shakes his head and starts walking again. I rush to keep up with him. Now it's my turn to ask, "What?"

"You really wanna know?"

I nod. Suddenly his opinion is very important to me.

"I'll tell you when you have a drink in you. I don't think you can handle this sober."

I follow him to El Charro. The place is famous for its nachos and margaritas. Suddenly, I'm famished. I feel as if I haven't eaten in—now that I think about it, I'm not sure the last time I did eat.

We head into the restaurant, the dim atmosphere finally dampening the bright glow of Thom's shirt. As we sit down, I inform Thom of my need to order food, especially if I need to drink.

"It's too late for me, but you go ahead."

"What do you mean, it's too late for you?" I look at my watch. It's a little after seven.

"Because I have to get up so early, my entire food schedule is shifted forward. I eat my first meal of the day at about five and my last at about five. I try to fast for twelve hours every day."

The statement seems so logical and organized, which surprises me. I look at Thom, with his bright shirts, spiky hair, and ever-present lollipop and devil-may-care attitude, and the last thing I expect is logic.

Perhaps appearances can be deceiving.

Hell, look at me: failed marriage, troubled children, absent mother, pillows for breasts. Nothing about me is what it seems.

"What?" I say finally, after the waitress has taken our drink orders. I can't bear the silence. Also, I can't fathom what he wants to talk about. I have no patience for this man. He brings out the absolute worst in me.

"You're a fool."

I open my mouth to protest, but he continues before I can get a word in. "Your ex is playing you for a fool. What night does he have the kids?"

"He's supposed to take them every other Sunday."

"Supposed to? What's that mean?"

Exactly what it sounds like. Other than Jordan's swim meets, Mike's probably only seen the kids once a month or so since he left.

It hasn't stopped him from texting me when he can't remember the name of his dry cleaner or what brand of socks he prefers. Because, of course, he has a sock preference.

It's the only time I hear from him. When he needs something from me. Something about him that I used to manage. I swear, the next time he contacts me, I'm going to tell him that Emily can figure this out for him.

"This is all new, and we're still navigating how it will all work. It's quite complicated."

The truth is, it's not, but there's no way in hell I'm admitting it out loud, least of all to Thom.

"Listen, Marg—you need to stand up for yourself. You've got to stop letting everyone, especially that douche waffle you were married to, walk all over you."

"I do not let everyone walk all over me!"

Mike is totally walking all over me.

Thom sits back, folding his arms across his chest. "Why are you here? You don't like me. Don't even bother trying to deny it. But you're here nonetheless. Why?"

I look at my hands, clenched tightly in my lap. Seriously, where is my margarita?

Finally, I clear my throat. "Because it would have been rude to refuse to come. Also, I was afraid that if I didn't come, I'd lose my job."

This startles Thom, causing him to push his chair back. "What?"

"I know Jack can't stand me, and you're the biggest talent there, so if you don't like me, then ..." I shrug. "And you have every reason not to like me. I've not been very nice to you. In fact, you seem to bring out the worst in me."

Thom holds up his hand. "You think I'll hold a grudge and get you canned if you don't go out with me? That's sexual harassment. How could you think I'd do that?" He's pissed.

Shame floods my chest. "Not *you* personally, but that's the way things work in the world. Why would people keep you around if you're not what they need?"

Like my father.

And my mother.

And my husband.

CHAPTER 19

"Dude, that is the most messed-up thing I've ever heard. Are you in counseling?"

"What?"

"You're all sorts of messed up. You know that, right?"

"I am not. I am together. I mean, look at me! Don't I look together?"

"Looks can be deceiving."

That's it. I slam my hands on the table and stand up. I've had about all I can handle of this man. He barely knows me, yet he continues to insult me by ... by ...

By saying the truth.

That realization wilts my knees, and I sink back into my chair.

"I'm not a mess."

Thom just cocks his head. "Would it be so bad if you were? Tacos are messy, but people love them nonetheless."

I narrow my eyes. "People are not the same as tacos. When you fall apart—hell, when you even start to crack—people put you down and walk away."

"So I take it you are not seeing a therapist."

He's like a dog with a bone. "No, and what's your deal with this anyway? Do you get a referral bonus or something?"

"No, it just seems like you have a lot going on. You break down in the group frequently. Maybe you need someone to talk to who knows what they're doing."

"I do not need a therapist. I'm fine."

"Talking about it helps."

"That's not how I'm wired. Talking about it does not help me."

The waitress finally brings our drinks and takes our order, providing a natural time to change topics. "I'm starving. I don't know the last time I ate."

Thom looks at me thoughtfully. I don't know what he's thinking, but I don't want him to tell me I need a shrink again, so I keep talking.

"This is good, because I haven't had much of an appetite. I can't resist the nachos here though. They're so good. I haven't had them in forever because, well, I was always watching what I ate. Now I have to gain weight for my surgery, if I even have it, so I have an excuse to have all the things I've denied myself for the past thirty-five years."

Thom's face is neutral, until I get to that last part. "How old are you?"

"Forty-five."

"So you've been on a diet since you were ten?" he scoffs.

I look into my drink. When I finally meet his gaze, he blanches. "No. Not really?"

I nod. "Nine, actually. My mom was just really getting going on dating, and it didn't look good to have a chunky daughter at home. Made her look like less of a catch, you know. As if the oily bohunks she picked up were actually interested in what I looked like."

"Your mom made you lose weight to make her more attractive to men? No wonder you're confused about people and their motives."

I shake my head. "It wasn't that. Not really. I mean, it was—partially."

"Partially?"

I sigh. The last time I told this story, it was to Mike and well before we were even engaged. I'd say it's not something I like to think about, but it's always there, running through my brain.

Large Marge.

"My name is Margot. My mom thought she was being fancy. My dad thought she was being pretentious, so from the day I was born, I was Margie. That quickly got shortened to Marge by the time I was in elementary school and my dad was long gone. Absent father, attention-seeking mother, and prepubescent hormones were enough to make me a little on the chunky side. That's all it took to get the nickname, Large Marge."

I can still hear the other fifth graders chanting it as I ate my bologna sandwich (on white bread, naturally).

White bread.

Between that and my mom's digs, it was enough to have me trying every fad diet in *Seventeen Magazine* and then *Cosmo*. In all honesty, once I hit puberty and grew six inches in a year, my weight was never an issue again.

Except for in my brain.

My poor body has been in a caloric deficit for so long that it probably thinks I'm starving to death.

"Wow. I didn't expect a bullying story."

"Yeah, well, I was all sorts of lucky growing up. You know, my dad left. My mom went from one man to another, desperate for someone who wouldn't leave her. It was easy to fall into that trap myself. When I was fifteen, I thought I'd found love with David Settles. Turns out, all I'd found was a creep who immediately told all his friends that we'd had sex. Overnight, I went from being Large Marge to Margot the Ho. I loved my childhood."

"So that's where Marg with a hard g comes from."

I shrug again. "I know it sounds terrible, but at least it doesn't rhyme with anything." I wipe a tear away. Kids can be so cruel.

"You wanna know why you can't call me Thom at the station?"

I nod, desperate for anything that isn't talking about my horrendous childhood.

"My last name is Jones."

"Okay."

"Think about it."

Thom ... Jones.

I shrug. "It's not unusual—"

He holds up his hand. "Stop!"

"What?" I ask innocently. "My grandmother was a big fan. You know what I always say about her? She's a lady." I can't help myself. "Whoa-oh-oh," I add on, singing off-key.

"This is why I go by TJ the DJ. Can you imagine the taunting and teasing I'd get working in radio?"

"Why would your mom do that to you?"

"She used to say that by spelling it with the h in there, which is totally dumb by the way, would differentiate me from Tom Jones."

I cock my head. "It's like a guy I dated in college. He was Mark, as was his roommate. When I said that it must get confusing when people called—this was back before cell phones, of course—he said no because his roommate was Marc with a c."

"Like you could hear the difference!" He laughs.

"I know, right? But there are so many other names. Why'd she saddle you with Thom?"

He shrugs. "Her maiden name was Thomas, and she wanted to see it carried on. She liked Thom better though, I guess."

"You guess? You should ask her what she was thinking."

"I would if I could, but believe me, if I only had one question for her, it would not be that."

Without even saying it, I know why Thom is in UnBRCAble. "How old were you when she—"

"Twenty. She was not quite fifty. Young and vibrant until cancer stole it from her. Back then, they didn't know about BRCA. She had battled cancer since she was thirty. You think when you are cancer free for ten years that you can relax. It turns out with BRCA-2, you can't ever relax. Her breasts were gone, but she still had a colon."

I wince, thinking back to that night when Thom gave me a ride home. I was awful, telling him he didn't have anything to worry about.

"You said you'd done one of those genetic tests and that's why you joined UnBRCAble."

He shrugs. "I wasn't sure how personal it got, so I held my cards to my chest."

Oh, it gets personal.

"Cancer sucks, man." I can't think of anything better to say.

"What about you?" he asks. "You've mentioned your mom."

"Yeah, my mom's fine. At least I think she is. She refused to get tested. She's in her early seventies now, with no signs of stopping. I'm not sure about my dad—I don't have much contact with him. Frankly, if it hadn't been for diligent self-checks, I don't know that I would have found anything."

"So you—"

I nod. "I found a lump. They biopsied it. There were precancerous cells but not enough to get anyone's panties in a twist. Well, not anyone but me.

Then they found another one. Stage one. Lumpectomy. Tamoxifen. I didn't want to keep going through this so I had the genetic testing done. I think everyone was shocked when I came back positive for the BRCA-1 mutation because I have no family history."

Thinking back, it was the first time Mike and I ever really went at it. He thought I was blowing it all out of proportion, but deep down in my gut I knew it was serious. "You know, Mike didn't want me to have the mastectomy at first. He thought I was being dramatic and attention-seeking. He asked the doctor if there could be a chance that I was losing my grip on reality."

"He sounds like a prince."

I smile and my shoulders drop a little. Maybe Thom isn't as bad as I thought he was.

I probably owe him an apology.

"It was hard for Mike to understand. It's hard for most people to understand. It's why I need the ladies in UnBRCAble. They don't think I'm crazy for having body parts removed. They know what it means to carry this threat on a daily basis."

Thom nods. He knows as well.

Okay, here goes. "I'm sorry for reacting the way I did when you first joined. I was caught off guard. I was also completely ignorant to the fact that just because you don't have ovaries doesn't mean you don't live facing the same threat that the rest of us do."

"Is that an apology?"

"Don't look so shocked. Contrary to what my douchebag ex says, I can admit when I'm wrong. It just didn't happen that much when it came to him."

"Except about him."

I raise my glass and tip it toward Thom. "Touché." I take a sip and then say, "I didn't even see it coming. I had no idea he found me so ... unpalatable. All I tried to do was everything right."

"Maybe you tried too hard."

"Too hard? Don't be ridiculous. There's no such thing as too hard in a marriage. Not enough, certainly. But not too hard. It takes a lot to make a marriage work. It's not like helicopter parenting. I may do too much for my kids, but I wasn't a helicopter wife. "

"Yes, and no one has ever accused me of working too hard. But it's late and this conversation could go on for a lot longer. Let's put a pin in it and we'll do this again sometime."

I glance at my watch. It's almost nine. I've never thought of nine as late, but I never thought I'd easily spend this much time talking to Thom either.

As soon as I'm in the car, my first instinct is to call Becky and tell her all about this. Instead, as I pull out my phone, what draws my eye are the notifications on the school app. Bailey hasn't turned in assignments in most of her classes in a few weeks.

Crap.

Just when I start to feel good about things, the rug is pulled out from under me. Why can't I catch a break?

CHAPTER 20

Breathe in. Breathe out. You cannot wring her neck.

Slowly, I exhale before opening the door to my daughter's bedroom. Not surprisingly, she's on her phone, TikToking away.

"Hey." I try to keep my voice light and neutral. "What's the homework situation?"

"All done. I did it in study hall." She doesn't even look at me, instead still gyrating away, making yet another video so her friends can tell her how awesome she is.

"Really? Do you do your homework in study hall most days? I don't see you spending much time on your stuff here."

"Un huh," she mumbles.

No way in hell am I going to tolerate her lying to my face. "Okay, I'll take the phone." I step into her room to take it, and she grasps it to her chest like a precious diamond.

"No."

No?

"Excuse me? Give me the phone."

She pulls it in closer, turning away. "No. You can't have my phone."

She bears a striking resemblance to Gollum. *My precious.*

"It's not your phone. You don't pay for it. Until you do, it's mine. And since you've decided not only to lie to my face but that you no longer need to do any schoolwork, I've decided to take your phone away."

I step to her with my hand out, yet she tightens her grasp. "No, you can't take it."

"Yes, I can, and if I have to pry it out of your hands, I will. Hand it over, now."

"It's not yours. You can't have it."

Her back talk is infuriating. She's always been headstrong, but this is ridiculous.

"Bailey, *give me the phone. NOW.*"

"No. It's not yours. You didn't pay for it either. Dad did. He's the only one who can take it away from me."

Not even when I found out Mike was cheating did I see red like I do in this moment.

I turn and walk away before I say something truly hurtful. But not before snatching the phone from her spoiled hands.

Because the thought that keeps running through my head is, "Yeah, but your father's not here now, is he?" She doesn't need to hear that. She knows it. She feels it acutely.

Something parents don't often consider is that when they leave their spouse for whatever reason, they are deserting their kids too. They may not mean to, but that's what happens.

And it leaves scars much deeper than the ones that march across my chest.

I want to remember that Bailey and Jordan are struggling too. I *need* to remember this. I've been so busy worrying about me that I didn't think about what this was doing to them. I mean, of course I did, but I also told myself that if I could just keep things going, maybe it wouldn't affect them that much.

Bailey's flunking school and Jordan's getting suspended for fighting.

I'm failing them.

"Family meeting time, right now," I yell. "In the kitchen."

Not surprisingly, Bailey's door stays shut. I knock once. Twice. Three times. "I know you're mad, but we need to talk. Now."

I head into the kitchen and start to make hot cocoa. I make it from scratch, the way I always have for the kids. The way I wish my mom would have taken the time to.

Jordan comes in, but still has the ever-present earbuds lodged firmly in place. I wonder if he even takes them out to shower. Finally, Bailey comes trudging in, a scowl etched on her young face.

You'd think she was headed to the guillotine rather than a family meeting.

"Okay listen, guys," I start, sliding a mug in front of each of them. Bailey's is her monkey mug and Jordan's looks like a lab beaker. He picked it out at the Museum of Science when he was nine, and it's been his favorite ever since. I wonder if either kid ever notices the details

I put into things. Like their preferred mugs and plates and utensils. Like the fact that Jordan has marshmallows while Bailey has whipped cream because it's what I know they like.

Mike doesn't know that.

And it's his loss, not mine.

"I know the last few months have been rough."

Bailey scoffs, "Yeah."

I ignore her. "This is not the way I saw things working out for any of us. Trust me, it's the last thing I wanted. I know what you're going through."

"Mom, you always say that, but you never do," Jordan says glumly.

This stops me short. "What do you mean?"

I see the kids exchange glances. Is this a thing between them that I don't know about? I didn't even think they really liked each other enough to have secret looks.

Still, neither kid answers. I prompt again, "What?"

Jordan takes a deep breath. "Mom, how can you know what we're going through? You didn't grow up with someone … like you as a mother."

I feel as if I've been punched in the gut. "Someone like me?" My voice is weak.

"Yeah," Bailey pipes in. "Gam is so cool. She'd never take my phone away."

"Gam," I say flatly.

"Yeah. Gam is a cool mom. Even though she's old and stuff, she's way cooler than you. She has a social life and—"

I hold my hand up. I don't want to hear any more. "My job is not to be cool. My job is not to be your friend. It's to make sure you both end up being the best, most responsible and decent human beings possible. I don't know that I've held you accountable enough. I—"

Jordan interrupts. "Yeah, Mom. We get it. Blah blah blah." He sounds just like his father.

He sounds just like his father.

"Fine. It's fine. It's all fine."

I stand up.

It's so not fine, and it never will be again.

"Mom ..." Bailey says slowly.

"Pack your bags. Call your father. Tell him to come get you. I'm done."

"Done?" Bailey repeats.

"Yes. I'm done with this family. You think I'm doing such a horrible job? Then go live with your father."

Bailey crosses her arms defiantly, jutting her chin out. "Fine. He'd let me have my phone."

Jordan's gaze darts back and forth between his sister and me. I know he's thinking about the urgent care visit, when his father wouldn't even take his calls. "Mom, you can't mean that."

"Why not? You think that you can treat me like garbage? That's what your father did. I don't have to— no, I *won't* stand for it from you. You don't like my rules, then you don't have to live in my house. So go." I snatch their hot chocolate from them, dumping it down the sink. I have half a mind to smash the mugs too, the way they've smashed my soul.

All I've ever wanted was to protect my children. To give them the love and security and approval I never had but so desperately sought.

And they took it without a thought or a care.

No one ever thought to love me back.

I hurry to my room, closing and locking the door behind me. I retreat farther into my bathroom, also locking the door. I don't know why I do this. It's not as if the kids will come in after me.

No one has ever come after me. I'm always the one running, begging to be loved.

Oh God, I'm just like my mother.

I pull out my phone. Before Becky can even say hello, I start. "I'm just like my mother."

"Too bold?"

"This is not the time for Prince lyrics. I thought I was so different than her. I tried to be. But I'm just like her," I ramble.

"Marg, slow down. What happened?"

"I told the kids to leave and go stay with Mike. All because they don't love and respect me. Why don't they love and respect me?"

"They do, but they're teenagers, so they're automatic buttholes. And you did not seriously tell them to go stay with Mike, did you?"

Shame fills me, causing my face to burn. I fill her in on the fight with Bailey over her grades and the lying and her phone. I tell her about the family meeting and the hot chocolate and Jordan's attitude. "He sounded just like Mike, and I snapped. They think I'm so terrible. I tried to extend the olive branch and neither one can see that I know what it's like to have your dad desert you. But still, they couldn't move one single centimeter toward meeting me halfway. I'm sick of being the villain in their story. In Mike's story."

"So how does this equate to you being like your mother?"

"Because all I want is for them to love me like I love them. That was the story of her life. It *is* the story of her life. She goes through every single day just desperate for people to love her. And I'm desperate for my kids to love me."

"You know I'm not going to blow smoke up your ass, right?" Becky is always frank with me, even when I don't want her to be.

"I'm counting on it."

"I don't think wanting your children to love and appreciate all you do for them is the same at all with what your mother does. Your mother seeks that from men. You don't."

"Yeah, fat chance of that with my situation." I glance down at my nonexistent rack. "Dating is so far off the radar it's on another screen."

"Some women have children because they want someone to love them. Some women have children because they have so much love to give. Your mother is the former, while you are the latter."

"But I'm upset that my kids don't love me." The tears erupt, spilling down my cheeks like a levy that busted under the storm surge.

"No, you're hurt because your kids are being rude, entitled dicks. They're lashing out at you because you're safe. You won't reject them like their father did. You can take it."

My stomach clenches. Oh no. "Except I didn't. I told them to leave."

"You told them if they didn't like your rules, they could leave."

I can't let them leave. Not like this.

Oh, my poor babies.

CHAPTER 21

As I come rushing out of my room, Jordan's shuffling awkwardly in the hall.

"Mom?" His voice is soft and reminds me of when he was little and would come into my room at night when he'd had a bad dream. "Do we really have to leave?"

"No, honey." I take him into my arms, my tears soaking his shirt. Even though he has about four inches on me in height and at each shoulder, he'll always be my little boy. "I'm sorry."

"I'm sorry too. I didn't mean it."

He abruptly lets go and turns away. Bailey calls down the hall, "Did you leave a message? Did he answer? Did he text back yet?"

The pain hits my heart as if a thoroughbred kicked my chest. Jordan's sorry only because his father is not there for him.

Again.

When Jordan turns and retreats to his room, Bailey crumbles, her face melting with anguish, the reality of the situation crashing down on her.

My poor baby.

I take her in my arms. She's never been a cuddler, and this moment is no different. She pushes me away. "I hate you. This is all your fault. You made Dad leave."

Even though her words aren't true, including her self-proclaimed hatred, they wound me nonetheless. And at least she's not internalizing Mike's desertion, blaming herself as I did when my father left.

Still, I wish I wasn't the cause of everyone's misery.

Unable to settle down, I head into the kitchen to clean up. At least that's a constant. No matter how bad my life is, there will always be dishes to be cleaned and counters to be wiped.

I wish crumbs would leave me the way everyone in my life seems to.

I sit at the counter, hating the cheap stools I bought off of Facebook Marketplace. There isn't enough padding and my hip bones ache. Someday, when I have the time and energy, I'll re-cover them, increasing the padding so my butt isn't sore.

It's like it's God's way of telling me I don't deserve to sit.

I stand up, the pressure easing on my rear. Immediately I feel better.

Huh.

I'm used to things aching and throbbing no matter what I do. I have tubes of Biofreeze and Voltaren and even some Aspercreme stashed everywhere. I have vibrating neck pillows and rice-filled sacks to heat in the microwave. I mainline ibuprofen to shush my aching bones.

Except I haven't used any of that recently.

I call Becky again. This time, she launches in. "How are things?"

"The kids are totally crushed because Mike didn't come swooping in to rescue them, and Bailey hates me for causing him to leave, so all in all, pretty normal."

"She doesn't hate you."

"I know she doesn't, but she's thirteen, so she probably feels like she does. But that's not why I called." I relay the story of the uncomfortable stools. "And I don't have any pain!"

"That's ... good?" she questions.

"Yeah. Remember I was getting headaches and things always hurt? I don't have that anymore. In fact, if my life weren't totally in the toilet, I'd say I feel good."

"That's weird."

"Right? Maybe I have some weird disease that attacked my pain sensors or something. I should Google it ..." I ponder.

"Or maybe you got so used to it that you don't even notice it anymore?"

Let's face it, that's the more reasonable answer.

"But I used to have it all the time, and I still noticed. I even put a tracker on my phone to keep tabs. My primary was going to send me to pain management if the headaches were severe enough. We talked about doing Botox in my neck for it. I was sort of hoping they could hook me up and give me a little in my forehead at the same time."

After we disconnect, I pull up the app and check my headache log. It's now the third week in March. My last recorded headache was the day I went in for surgery, almost three months ago.

That can't be right.

I'm sure I slacked off in those post-op days because I was on pain medication. But surely I've had a headache since?

I think about it, the past few months whirling through my mind like a VHS cassette on rewind.

No headaches. No brain fog. No missed appointments or forgotten things.

All this despite being one of the most stressful times of my life.

Huh.

It's like in exchange for complete and total life turmoil, God took away the feeling of general malaise and poor health that had plagued me for the past few years.

My pain left with my boobs.

My pain left with my boobs.

Well now crap.

I Google "implant illness." Sure enough, I had most of the symptoms. Joint pain. Chronic fatigue. Sleep disturbance. Gastrointestinal distress (though a lady doesn't talk about such things). Concentration problems. Memory problems. Anxiety. Depression. Headaches.

I could be the poster child for breast implant illness.

How did I not see it before? I mean, when it's come up in UnBRCAble before, I just assumed it was something that happened to other people. You know, like cheating spouses.

I'd had my implants for so long that it never occurred to me I could have this.

I should have known my body would conspire against me, attacking my breast implants. Hell, my body is genetically wired to kill me, so why would this surprise me?

Maybe it was just because they were the textured kind and defective to begin with. Maybe the smooth kind will be okay. I can't believe I have to wait a full week to bring this up in UnBRCAble. We've talked about implant illness before. Someone has got to have the answers.

~~~**~~~

Turns out, I've found the answers.

They are not the answers I want.

I could do what Mike used to do. If he asked a question and didn't like the answer he received, he'd keep asking and asking, hoping that eventually he'd hear what he wanted to hear.

That's sort of laughable because it's obvious he always heard what he wanted to hear.

I leave Dr. Chung's more defeated than I've been in a while, which is saying a lot.

The rest of last week sucked, and the weekend sucked even more. The only thing that was keeping me going was the hope of good news at this appointment.

The kids are miserable. Bailey mostly because she doesn't have her phone back. She's like an addict going through withdrawal. No lie, I found her in the fetal position on her floor.

The phone loss is probably a good thing. She needs a separation from it.

Jordan's mood, on the other hand, is not a good thing. The anger, which is totally appropriate and expected, is wafting off him in waves.

I miss the good old days when the only thing wafting off him was too much Axe body spray.

As I find myself doing more and more these days, I take an extra moment in the car, mentally coaching myself to put on my big-girl panties and face the day.

In reality, I have the vents on high, pointing at my face to dry the tears before they stain my cheeks. I can't let anyone know that I sit in my car and cry like this.

I unplug my phone from the car charger and prepare to put it in my purse. As I do, I see that I have a friend request ... from Thom.

Huh.

Well, I guess we are friends, so I accept. While I'm holding the phone, it rings. Continuing to scroll through my feed, I answer using the steering wheel controls.

It's Becky. "How'd you make out?"

Trying to still look at Facebook while picking up my coffee, I nearly drop my phone.

"Oh shoot. Dropped my phone. Okay, I got it. I just pulled into work, but I needed a minute to pull myself together. You know, I bet Mike never has to sit in his car, trying to gather himself before he can go into work. He never needs a moment to stuff everything back down so he can look put together when in reality his world is falling apart. He never had to stand in the shower, crying silently so the kids couldn't hear."

"I'm not sure men ever do."

Even before my marriage crumbled, Becky had been my person for years. She's always been here to listen to me, as I do for her. Today is no different. She is my safe space, and I use it to rant, unleashing the pain and anger that's been building inside me like a pressure cooker.

Not one of those safe Instapots either, but the old-school, blow-the-top-off kind.

"It's shit, really. My life. I worked so hard to have what I wanted in life. You know, what's the line of bull they sell you? Work hard and you can have it all. Prince Charming will come and sweep in and you'll live happily ever after in your castle, but also with your high-powered career. If you want it, you can have the ball gowns as well as the power suits. Well, guess what? You can't have it all. I went to school, studied hard. I found a man who told me he didn't believe in divorce and that I was the most important thing in his life. That family was the most important thing to him. I gave up the possibility of a career to raise my kids, and I did so because it was important. I've wiped asses and snotty noses. I've cleaned up puke and poop. Hell, I clean every freaking day. I don't think that anyone in my house even knows where I keep the mysterious device known as the vacuum, and don't get me started on wiping down the counters. I cook gourmet meals for my kids. I exercise, watch what I eat, do my research, and try to be the best mother and person I can be. I try so hard. God. Every day, all I do is try."

Tears well up, but I don't bother wiping them away.

"And where does it get me? I'm sitting in my car, trying not to ugly cry before I go into work because you know what I look like when I ugly cry. And what do I have to cry about? Let me list the ways. I survived my father walking out, my mother neglecting me in lieu of dating, and horrendous bullying in my childhood. I can't even use my real name because of the torment I felt. But I endured and survived, and it was okay because I finally had the perfect life. Perfect until breast cancer and faulty genetics swooped in and stole my breasts and ovaries and hormones. Perfect until my husband decided that the work I put into making our perfect home and life was too much for him to deal with, and he left me for some floozy, and now I have no way to meet the mortgage payment or pay for college in two years. I have to drive a Kia now! We've been together for twenty years, and now the only time I hear from him is when he texts me to find out what brand of oatmeal he likes. Now I'm working for basically minimum wage because dedicating your life to your children and volunteering doesn't count as experience, and no one will hire you if you've only worked part-time for the past decade. I can raise people but that doesn't qualify me to answer phones at a school, despite the fact that I have a bachelor's degree in accounting."

I'm on a roll.

"And let's talk about those people I raised. My kids are entitled brats who are driving head-first off the rails. How did I not notice what a-holes they were turning into? So all I have left is me. But what is that really? A body that is genetically wired to develop cancer. Breast implants that not only can cause me to get another type of cancer but that also cause my body to attack itself, making me sick every single day of my life. Dr. Chung just told me I can never get new implants because I will always get sick from them. I am probably not a candidate for other reconstruction because of years of dieting—as a result of that bullying from both peers and my mother—have left me too thin to be able to create new breasts from my fat cells. Not that I can have that surgery anyway because my health insurance is shit. I can't afford it, nor can I afford to take the time off from my craptastic job. My ex-husband has totally deserted his kids, and I don't have anyone who will take care of me while I recover from the surgery. So, basically, I have to go through life stuffing my bra like a twelve-year-old. But it's not supposed to matter, right, because at least I survived my cancer to live a long, sort-of healthy life. Alone. How am I ever supposed to feel attractive again? I can never date. Mike is out there with a steaming hot love life while I'm destined to a life of high necklines, oversized shirts, and spinsterhood because no one would ever want to date a woman without breasts. It's probably not even really a loss. I mean, since the hysterectomy to prevent me from getting ovarian cancer, it's not like I have much of a sex drive anyway. Things are drier than the Sahara down there anyway. Not exactly prime real estate for someone to want to set up shop, if you know what I mean. I'm forty-five years old, and I'm tired. So tired. Tired of the mental load of parenting. Tired of being the default parent. Tired of trying to run a dog and pony show so my kids don't notice that their father is a piece of shit and deserted them. I know what that feels like, and I never wanted them to feel that way. But instead of falling apart, or running off, I've got to pull myself together and go in to a boss that desperately needs my skills but hates me nonetheless. I've worked my whole life to be perfect, and my whole life is a steaming pile of crap. The only thing I'm perfect at being is a failure."

I exhale, feeling as if a weight has been lifted off my chest.

That felt good.

Sometimes you need to explode to be able to pull it all together again.

"Thanks for listening, Beck. I needed to get that off my chest. I've got to get inside. I'll call you later."

I shove my phone into my purse and take a deep, cleansing breath in. I'm not even through the parking lot when my phone rings. I glance quickly in my open bag. It's Becky. She probably just butt-dialed me. I swipe dismiss and continue on. About thirty seconds later, the phone rings again. I'm walking through the door, so I ignore it.

When the phone rings as I'm approaching my desk, I pull it out. "I just got to my desk. Can I call you later? I get fifteen in about four hours," I whisper.

"Oh shit, Marg. You just livestreamed that whole rant on Facebook."

CHAPTER 22

No. No. No. No. No.

"What do you mean?"

I swipe up and see that yes, indeed, I am live on Facebook. "Eep!" I yell as I hurry to end the video.

The twelve-minute video.

Oh. My. God.

A string of expletives runs through my brain. And maybe out of my mouth a little.

What did I even say during that rant?

I sink down into my chair, my knees weak and my stomach threatening to return its contents with velocity.

Three views. Five views. Seventeen views.

Oh God.

As fast as I can coordinate my shaking fingers, I delete the post.

My Messenger starts pinging. Great.

Maybe I can figure out the seventeen people who saw it and apologize. I should have watched it before I deleted it so I knew what I said.

I remember some of it, and it wasn't good.

I put my head on the desk and slowly start banging it. At least it was contained to a handful of people. It could have been so much worse.

Slowly, I straighten up. It could have been worse. No one is going to see it. I quickly type out a message to my cousin who was one of the seventeen.

"Whoops, sorry for that. Obviously, I didn't know I was broadcasting. You caught me in a pity-party for one. I'm fine. Thank you for your concern, and I'm sorry for the things I said."

Okay, time to move on. To do better. To be better.

You know, the story of my life.

I take one last deep, cleansing breath before I turn my attention to work. We have three promotional appearances this week. I have to finish coordinating the details as well as put together a list of prizes to pull from the swag room and mail out to contestant winners.

Did I mention that due to my organization system in that room I've received added responsibilities?

Awesome.

I'm too upset to sit and focus on details, so instead I start with the prizes. An hour later, they're packaged up and ready to go. "I'm running to the post office!" I call out, a stack of padded envelopes balanced precariously in my arms. The nice thing about not really having breasts is that I can hold too many things more securely with less of a chance of dropping them.

It's one bright side, I guess.

I get to the post office, stacking up the packages again, and use my butt to open the door. As I push in, I hear the laughter coming through the loudspeakers.

It's the Morning Meltdown with TJ the DJ and Todd.

"Okay, so let's talk about the women in our lives. I'm currently looking for the next ex-Mrs. TJ, so Todd, tell me about your wife. Is she frazzled?"

"No, man, she's got it together."

"Yeah, she's lying to you."

"What? No. Krista is cool, calm, and collected. She has it all under control. The house, the kids, everything. She runs the show."

TJ laughs. "It's a ruse, man. Krista—and no disrespect, Krista, because you know I love you for putting up with this oaf—does not have it together. At any moment, she is one snap of the fingers away from losing her stuff. Totally going off the deep end. It's okay that you didn't know, Todd. Apparently, it's a big secret that women keep from us. They routinely emasculate men by showing them up. Women are so good at juggling everything. They make it look so easy. And *it's all a lie*."

I roll my eyes. TJ the DJ is so full of hot air, it's not even funny. What does he know about women?

"TJ, where you getting this from?"

"So I know this woman ..."

"I'll bet you do." Todd's voice is full of innuendo. I'm sure Thom gets around—he's a minor celebrity—but having spent some time with him, I can't picture him dating. Despite his on-air persona, he doesn't seem like a player.

"No, it's not like that. Not with this woman. She's too out of my league. She's got it all together. Her life is like literally falling apart, and she still shows up and runs things around here like a freakin' professional, man. She's done more in the last month than anyone has done here in a decade. She could probably take over this place and in three weeks would not only have the entire station organized but could probably do the airtime too. All in her sleep."

Todd laughs. "I know who you're talking about, and you're right. Classy lady. Totally put together."

"Totally. But here's the thing: she's a liar. She lets us *think* that she's got it under control, but really—she's just a hot mess like the rest of us."

"No."

"Yes."

"How did you find this out?"

"So this is the best part. She broadcasted a Facebook Live."

Oh shit.

"I don't think she knew she was live though. I suspect she was talking to someone. But man, she let it all out. *All out.*"

"Dude."

"Right? But I feel so deceived. I see her all the time, and there's nothing she can't do. Or that's what it seems like. But in reality, she's drowning, just like the rest of us."

"She can't be," Todd says. "No way."

"Way."

"Can't be. I don't believe you, TJ."

A roar floods my ears, panic rushing through me. Oh my God. Oh my God. Thom saw it. He knows. He sees my mess.

My imperfections.

And he's telling the world about it.

I need to get back to the station to stop this. The line finally moves though. I can't leave without sending these prizes out.

No matter what personal hell I'm in, I still have a job to do. After all, how will people live without their free T-shirts and signed pictures?

Bile is rising up the back of my throat, and had I eaten anything before my appointment with Dr. Chung this morning, there's a good possibility I would be throwing up everywhere.

This feeling is as bad as when I found that text on Mike's phone.

Actually, it's worse.

That rant that only my best friend in the world was supposed to hear is out there with someone who broadcasts to thousands of people every day. Becky has been with me since the Large Marge days and was my only friend during the Margot the Ho period. She remembers Stepdads Two, Three, and Four, and the epic disappointment that was my father. She knows *me* in a way that no one else does.

I don't need to be perfect for her. She loves me for who I am, ugly spots and all.

God only knows why.

She must be defective because no one who has ever seen my flaws has stayed around to love me. And now, TJ the DJ is telling the whole world about how broken I am. He's probably going to post the video to his website.

I'm surprised he didn't mention the boob thing.

Oh my God, what if he says on air that I have no breasts and wear stuffing to make it look like I do?

I would never, ever be able to leave the house again.

Rushing out of the post office, I hightail it back to the station, my fingers fumbling with the radio tuner. I usually listen to satellite radio, so it takes me a minute to find WBRC the Rock. It's double play Monday, so I've got at least two songs before Big Mouth Thom gets back on the air.

They play two by R.E.M. and then start in with Oasis. Normally, I'd sit and listen, enjoying the nostalgia to my college days when I played, (What's the Story) Morning Glory? on repeat. No today. I've got to get inside.

Like something out of a bad movie, I attempt to exit my car without undoing the seat belt first. I drop my purse, the contents spilling out into the parking lot. Quickly, I scoop them back up and hustle into the building.

Without stopping, I walk—even though I want to run—to the studio hallway. Outside the door, I stop, taking a deep breath. I don't know what I'm going to say to him.

I don't have time to figure it out. "Champagne Supernova" is about seven minutes long, and it's already on the guitar exit.

Smudge the Producer looks up, startled, as I fling the door open. I don't actually know what his name is, as he's only ever referred to as Smudge the Producer, much like Thom is only ever called TJ the DJ. It doesn't matter. All that matters is that I have to stop TJ.

Through the window, I can see TJ and Todd sitting at a long table, spaced about six feet from each other. I always pictured them huddled close, so it surprises me that they are so far apart. On the table between them are countless devices and screens, piles of paper, and at least six coffee mugs. There are three plates of pastries and doughnuts. There are panels of buttons that must do complicated things, and behind TJ is a massive wall of CDs.

I didn't think anyone used them anymore.

Todd is stretched out in his chair, his hands folded across his ample midsection, and his head resting back. His mouth is open, lending to the very real possibility that he's sleeping. The only thing that indicates he may actually be working is his headset. Littered around him on the floor are at least a dozen wads of paper.

Thom looks up, the grin fading instantly from his face. He holds up a finger telling me to wait and presses a few buttons. The acoustic guitar chords of "Wonderwall" begin. Thom slides his headset down and waves me in.

With Liam Gallagher's gravelly voice as the backdrop, I finally say, "How could you?" I swallow hard, as if the movement in my throat can push down the tears in my eyes.

"I—you blew me away with that Live. I know you've been struggling, but here at work, you have your shit so together. No one would ever know."

I don't hear his compliments. "And now everyone knows."

"No one knows. Except maybe Todd and well ..." Thom looks over at him and shrugs. He picks up a piece of paper from in front of him and wads it up, lobbing it at his co-worker who is indeed sleeping.

"How could you? Why would you do that to me?"

"Margot, please, calm down. I ... we had a guest no-show this morning, and so we were ad-libbing for filler. I saw your video. I had to put on some extended plays just to watch it all. And as I was watching, it hit me that men have *no idea* what women go through trying to run the house. Trying to raise a family. You come in here every day so cool, calm, and collected. No one would ever guess what a mess you are underneath it all. You are efficient and professional, and you have this place running better than it ever has. Our ratings are up two and a half points since you started. You are a machine. Yet you are totally falling apart. How do you do it?"

I open my mouth to answer and then close it when I don't know what to say.

Thom holds up his finger again, wadding up another ball of paper and this time hitting Todd right between the eyes. "And that was two from Oasis. I've heard Noel Gallagher say repeatedly that he was high when he wrote all their songs. We should get him on here and see if he can explain what exactly a 'Wonderwall' is. What do you think, Todd? Smudge the Producer, see what you can do about booking Noel Gallagher."

"What about Liam? He's the interesting one," Todd chimes in. "But I don't know that booking either of them is good, unless we book them together."

"Man, they hate each other."

I stand there, paralyzed and silent, as they banter back and forth. They are live on the air, and if I say anything, everyone in the world will hear.

My stomach tightens and rumbles, protesting the missed breakfast. My hands fly to my abdomen, as if covering it can stop that loud noise from reverberating through the booth.

A small smile seeps through Thom's mouth. He leans forward and slides a plate toward me.

"I'm not sure how we'd do an on-air interview," Todd says. "Every televised interview with them I've ever seen had subtitles to understand them."

"Don't they speak English? They're British." Thom nods at me, pushing the plate more toward me, even while he continues speaking. Silently, I take a cheese danish. "Why subtitles?"

Todd answers, never showing signs that he was sleeping two minutes ago. "Their accents are so thick that us dumb Americans can't understand what they are saying. Either that or they were so high and drunk none of what they were saying made sense."

"That could be a real possibility. Todd, we've got to take a short break. What double play do you want to hear after a word from our commercial sponsors?"

Todd looks at me and winks. "We have a special guest in our studio right now. Let's ask her."

Crap. Crap. Crap.

Thom nods reassuringly. "Lady K, who organizes everything here for us, is in the studio, stealing a pastry. If you come to see anyone from the station at a live event, the only reason it runs like a well-oiled machine is Lady K here, so we let her take the good pastries. So, Lady K, what do you want to hear?"

The cheese danish is suddenly sawdust in my mouth. How can he be talking to me like this? Chatting as if he didn't just betray me for the world to hear? Doesn't he know how much he hurt me?

"Hurt." The word flies out before I can stop it.

"Never pictured you for a Nine Inch Nails fan, but we can roll with it."

I find my voice, not that the listeners will be able to hear. Thom turns his mic toward me. "Actually, I like the Johnny Cash version better than Nine Inch Nails, but that may not fit in with the station's master playlist."

Todd perks up. "No, man, the Johnny Cash version is better. There, I said it. Trent Reznor, come after me."

Thom swings the mic back toward him so he can talk. "You know, Lady K, this is right up your alley. I read a story about Trent Reznor doing the preschool drop-off and PTO thing. Can you imagine if your kids' perfect

PTO had the lead singer from Nine Inch Nails in it? Lady K, what would you do?" The mic is back pointing at me.

What's with the Lady K crap? My eyes widen, and I don't have time to think. I say the most honest thing that pops into my brain. It's like being around Thom makes me lose that social filter that I apply in more layers than an Instagram influencer. "Listen, as long as he was volunteering and not complaining, I wouldn't say anything. That's the worst part of doing something like the PTO. No one wants to show up and do the hard work, but then everyone has an opinion on how you should have done it. I don't care who he is as long as he volunteers for the spring carnival."

I feel something closing in on my head. I look to see Smudge the Producer sliding a set of headphones on me. There's also a chair right behind me. His hands push slightly down on my shoulders, guiding me to sit.

"So put up or shut up, then?" Thom asks, leaning into the mic which is now in the middle of the table for us to share.

"Pretty much. That, and I'd probably always have some inappropriate lyrics running through my head whenever I saw him." I relax down into the chair and stop gripping the edge of the table. "On the other hand, I'm of a certain age demographic that would know who he is. Most parents of younger kids would have no idea. He's got that going for him, that he's a lot older than the other parents."

Todd laughs, his booming voice coming through my earphones. "You gotta point there. We'll be back with The Man in Black in five minutes."

Then, there's silence. Thom slides his headphones down and motions for me to do the same.

"You were great, Margot. A total natural. I mean, I shouldn't be surprised now, should I? There's nothing you can't do."

Thom is smiling and relaxed. Almost like he didn't just talk about me on the air—again—airing my dirty secrets and then put me on the spot like that.

I hold up my hand, standing up abruptly. "No, don't even think about it."

"Think about what?" He rises too.

"Acting like you're my friend. What you did just now—today as a whole—was wrong. You're not my friend. You're an opportunist who will exploit my every weakness for your own personal gain."

Without waiting for him to respond, I leave the booth.

See, this is what happens when you let someone in on your vulnerable side. They use it and abuse it, and then they let you go.

Just when I thought Thom might even be my friend, he has to prove my theory right.

CHAPTER 23

Thom is everywhere. At work. On air. Billboards and the sides of buses.

And, of course, UnBRCAble.

We don't have an ethics code here, but I'm wondering if we need to get one. I get to the meeting early so I can talk to Claudia.

"Did you see the pictures Erin posted on Facebook? I swear, that squishy little bundle of pink is almost enough to make me want to have a baby." Claudia's face lights up. "Almost."

As adorable as Erin's daughter Eleanor is—and how much I would love to squeeze her chubby cheeks—I can't get distracted from telling Claudia how Thom is violating our code of honor in UnBRCAble.

I'm pretty sure we have a code of honor here. If not, we totally should.

"I'm a little concerned about Thom being in the group."

Claudia sighs.

"No, wait, hear me out. I know I was not the most receptive when he first joined. I was not showing my best self and did not welcome him the way that is expected in this supportive group. I was quick to judge, and I judged for erroneous reasons. However, the results of my conclusion may not be entirely incorrect."

"How so?" Claudia takes off her coat and tosses it on the back of her chair. I hang mine up carefully.

"Right after Thom joined, he presented my objection to him joining on his radio show, which resulted in his audience agreeing with him that I was a 'jerk-face'." I make the little quote signs with my fingers. "It really hurt to hear what happened in this group played out to the public. As I'm sure you know, I work for Thom's radio station."

I relay to her the story of the Facebook Live and Thom's resultant discussion about it on air. "I mean, he obviously knew I didn't mean to broadcast it, and so it was totally uncalled for him to bring it up."

Claudia nods. "Well, I can see why you're upset. However, it's not like Thom was revealing specific or identifying details about you in either case. I will say something tonight, but I don't think there is any reason that Thom can't be here."

Other than I don't want to be anywhere near him.

I sit down, crossing my arms over my chest. Internally I'm 'harrumphing,' but I don't dare express disapproval out loud. No one likes a person with sour grapes.

And man, are my grapes sour.

Thom enters, late as usual, and sits down *next to me*. Like we're friends or something. It is taking everything I have not to rip that stupid lollipop out of his mouth and whack him on the head with it.

I feel almost as much animosity toward him as I do toward Mike. Thom is the personification of everything I've worked my entire life to get away from. He's a fly-by-the-seat-of-his-pants guy with no regard for rules and order. He puts his own needs first, everyone around him be damned.

And he always wears those ugly Hawaiian shirts.

My anger is growing and festering, bubbling up like a soup left on too long. There's a very good chance I may explode.

"Marg?"

I look up. Claudia's obviously asked me something, if the concerned look on her face is any indication.

"I'm so sorry. What?"

"I'd asked if anyone else had anything they need to talk about. Thom thought you might."

I glare at him. How dare he? How—oh wait, I do need to talk about something. I almost let my anger supersede my need to discuss my health.

I will not let some stupid man cost me anything else.

"Dr. Chung thinks I have implant illness. Or had, I guess, since my symptoms have almost totally vanished since I had the implants removed."

"What made him think about BII?" Kelli asks. I feel bad for bringing it up with her here. She's still presurgical, mostly because she's terrified of things going wrong. And I'm the poster child for wrong.

"Um, I asked. I used to have terrible headaches, and a bunch of other things too."

"Like what?" Kelli asks eagerly. Oh boy. This is like telling a labor and delivery story in front of a newly pregnant woman. No good can come of this. She must sense my hesitance. "Please? I want to know so I can make a really informed decision."

"Well, in addition to the headaches, there was the joint pain, debilitating fatigue, memory problems, anxiety, depression, difficulty concentrating, and, uh"—I glance at Thom and hold up my finger in a warning—"diarrhea. Every single day. I don't think I've had any since I had them removed."

Kelli's face is a few shades paler than when we started.

"You know, they were all little things that I barely noticed, but now that they're gone, I feel so much better. I've even lost weight without trying, though that's not really a good thing right now."

"So what are you going to do?" Kelli's pupils are as big as saucers.

I shrug. "I don't know. The doctor doesn't think putting any kind of implants back in is the best choice. At least not for several years. He thinks my body needs that much time to heal so it doesn't react. In theory, the best option is the DIEP flap reconstruction, but I can't keep enough weight on. Also, I don't really have the support that I will need to go through with that surgery and recovery." I shrug again, unsure of what else to say.

Tracey says, "Have you ever considered staying flat?"

Now my eyes are the ones as wide as saucers.

"Flat? Hell no."

Tracey holds her hands up like she's surrendering. "I don't think I could either. Especially not in your situation. I mean, dating in your forties is bad enough. Dating without boobs? You might as well wait for pigs to fly."

Tracey's right. Dating's been a struggle for her with her reconstruction. Her man from New Year's is long gone.

"Honestly, I can't even think about dating. I was with Mike for so long ... it would be weird."

"You aren't waiting for him to come back, are you?" Millie asks. The concern on her face is genuine because, well, that's how Millie is.

"Never. I am the most loyal person you've ever met, until you screw me over. Then"—I glance sideways at Thom—"you're dead to me."

"Oh, phew," Millie sighs. "I didn't know what to say to you or how you felt about him. Sterling said he's been a total jack-hole lately."

"That would be Mike. But trust me, dating is the last thing on my mind right now. My kids and my health are a lot more important than some stupid man."

There's some applause, and even an "Amen, sister" from someone in the group. As quiet descends, Thom says, "I think you should consider staying flat."

And that does it.

I stand up and hiss, "And I think you should never, ever, comment on anything to do with my body ever again. It is none of your business. Stay out of my life and stay far away from me."

I storm over to the closet area and have to pull my coat one, two, three times to get it off the hanger. My dramatic exit would have been so much easier if I had just thrown my coat over the back of my chair.

When will I learn that following the rules never helps me out?

Once I make it to my car, I'm so angry that I am shaking. Then the tears come. God, this is all so unfair. I call Becky and tell her what Thom said, this time double—and triple—checking to make sure I'm not broadcasting live.

"He has no right to comment on my body!"

There's silence on the line.

"What?"

"Isn't Thom a member of the group?"

"Yeah. That's where all my problems started."

Becky sighs. "You know I love you, and I know you love me. Please know I'm coming from a good place when I say this. Also, I don't want to fight, so I'm going to say my piece and then hang up so you can think about it without arguing with me about it."

This is not going to be good. But I trust Becky with my life. "If you think I need to have a come-to-Jesus moment, so be it. Lay it on me."

"Your problems didn't start with Thom. They didn't even start with Mike. They started with your parents and your messed-up childhood. Thom is not your problem. If Claudia or Millie or Erin had said the same thing to you, you'd have heard them and talked about it. Instead you melted down. Again. I think you're blaming all your daddy issues on Thom, and he's really an innocent bystander. Okay, gotta go, love you, bye."

And then the line disconnects.

It's a good thing too, because excuse me? Daddy issues?

~~~***~~~

I'm still fuming the next morning when I drive into work. Out of some sort of morbid curiosity, I turn the satellite radio off and tune into WBRC the Rock to see what TJ the DJ and Todd are saying.

I'm a glutton for punishment.

Today they're yammering on about some hockey game that was on last night, then segueing into a conversation about some movie Todd watched. The two topics aren't at all related, but I'm amazed at how seamlessly they transition from one to the other. Then they mention that after the next song, they'll be talking to the star of that movie.

If I didn't know better, I'd think this was carefully scripted by a skilled team of writers. Instead I know Todd is in between catnaps and Thom's mind is like a whirling dervish that never stops, thinking of new ways to make my life hell.

Seriously though, I wonder if Todd has sleep apnea or narcolepsy or something? He might want to get checked out. If I'm nothing, it's an advocate for proactive healthcare.

As Pearl Jam's "Black" begins to play, I wonder if Thom somehow knows I'm listening. This song sums up my mood perfectly. Oh, Eddie Vedder, you've said it all.

But instead of thinking about Mike, who I should be thinking about, my father pops into my head. Like in the song, he seems to have an influence, like a faint tattoo, on everything in my life. His absence was so much more prevalent than his presence. He started taking off when I was six. Gone for good by the time I was eight. It's been close to forty years of not having him in my life on a regular, dependable basis.

I stopped wishing he'd come back.

Hoping … that's another story.

If only I was prettier, maybe he'd have wanted to stay. If I was a boy. If only I was neater or did my chores without being asked. If only I didn't scream when Arlo bothered me. If only I didn't ask him to play with me when he came home from work.

As the song winds down and TJ the DJ and Todd come back on, ramping up for their special guest, I literally shake my head to get out of my funk.

Okay, so I'm a little messed up because my dad left. It doesn't mean I have daddy issues. It certainly doesn't mean that I'm falling apart because of them.

No, I have a lot on my plate.

But it's time for me to stop making excuses and get myself back together. I have standards for living.

I haven't been holding myself to those standards, with my outbursts and anger.

No, I can't let that out anymore. No one wants to be around someone who lashes out.

No one wants to be around someone who is judgmental.

I want to be a person that people want to be around.

I need to try harder to be better.

Okay. I can do this.

I square my shoulders and park the car. Today is the first day of the rest of my life, and I'm bound and determined to make the best of it.

CHAPTER 24

"No."

So much for my resolve to be my best self, but this is a whole lotta nope.

"Yes."

"No. Absolutely not. No way."

Thom leans in and whispers, "It's literally your job to say yes. Your *actual* job. Read the description."

I sigh. He's not wrong, but I'm not going to admit he's right either.

"Fine, get in."

He's not wrong that when I'm driving to an event—this time a live broadcast from a mall as a fundraiser for the Red Cross—I have to transport the talent. I get to drive the station's Ford Explorer to haul the booth setup and swag there. It's also my responsibility to load and unload all the stuff, as well as make sure there's gas in the SUV. Usually the talent gets there on their own. I drove Mike Mitchell one time to a car dealership, but it turns out that he's a functioning alcoholic and really shouldn't be driving. Ever.

Thom's never asked me to drive him. He and Todd usually arrive together.

After a few tense moments of silence, I have to know why he's tormenting me. "Why?"

"Why what?" he asks, slowly pulling the lollipop out of his mouth. I swear his teeth are going to rot out of his head with all that sugar constantly in his mouth.

"Why did I have to drive you?"

"Todd is meeting us there. He had something to do first, so he couldn't bring me. And it's your job. You wouldn't want to let me down, would you?"

Damn it, he knows my Achilles' heel.

I give him a quick side-eye before returning my gaze to the road.

"Plus, I never drive to these things in my car. It's too conspicuous."

"That it is."

"Once people know that I drive it, they can identify me out and about town. This protects my privacy."

"Privacy … I'm so glad you value it." Like his Hawaiian shirts don't announce his presence with a scream.

"I'm detecting a little sarcasm here."

"Good to know. I'd be worried about you if you couldn't sense my animosity."

"I didn't violate your privacy."

"Um, yeah, you did. Twice you've talked about me on the radio. Private things. And now the whole world knows."

"The world does not know. No one knows who you are. They don't even know that the woman who got the Jerk-Face Award was the same woman who did the accidental livestream. In both cases, you're an anonymous person who could be anyone. The only one who will destroy that anonymity is you."

One of the things I hate most about Thom is when he uses logic and reason to destroy me.

I also hate that for some reason, unbeknownst to me, I lose all of my composure and poise around him. I'd never rant and rave at someone the way I do him. I was probably with Mike for at least five years before I ever lost it on him the way I do with Thom. And even then, it's probably only been a handful of times.

It's like I'm the anti-Marg with Thom.

"So if you value your privacy so much, why do you drive that car around? It's so ... so ..." I search for the appropriate word.

"Awesome. It's a 1970 Oldsmobile Custom Coupe."

He may as well be speaking in gibberish. "My dad bought it for my mom when they were first married. She didn't learn how to drive until then, so he bought that for her as a present."

It was his mom's first car.

"Oh. But it's so ..." Once again, I'm at a loss for words. Tacky? "Muscle car-y," I finally come up with. "It's not a girl car. Or a mom car. It's a car for a man with a small penis or IQ." A soon as the words leave my mouth, I wish I could pull them back in.

I should have just said tacky.

This is so not like me. I'm not a ready-fire-aim person. No one likes people without a filter.

"I can assure you that is not the case here, either with myself or with my dad. My mom saw the car and fell in love. My dad would have moved Heaven and Earth to make her happy. It didn't matter that she couldn't drive yet. And that car made her happy. In turn, it makes me happy to think of her when I drive it. But it does allow people to identify me easily, and I don't want that."

"I'm so sorry. I didn't mean to say such a rude thing," I mumble.

"Yes, you did, and don't apologize. You've been thinking about my junk so own it."

My face flushes hot. "No, I haven't. I've thought that you had to be compensating, but good God, no. I haven't been thinking of you like that."

To quote Cher Horowitz, as if.

"Why not? I'm a good-looking guy. Easy to get along with. I mean, easy for everyone except you."

I glance over to see him shrug. I also see the grin on his face and realize he's teasing me.

"You're kidding."

"Of course I'm kidding, except not about size and the fact that I'm good-looking. Margot, you really need to lighten up. Maybe laugh a little. You know, when you're not overthinking things, you can be pretty funny. You just need to let loose."

Un huh.

"I don't think I need a lecture from you on social decorum or how to act. I'm good."

"But that's the thing. You're not. Don't forget—I saw your Facebook Live. You are barely holding it together. And with good reason. But something's gotta give, sooner or later. Wouldn't it be better to control what you let go of rather than have it spiral away, out of your control?"

Fortunately, we arrive at the mall, so I don't have to continue this conversation. Like there's any way I'm going to let loose.

I let loose with David Settles and was labeled a slut for the rest of high school. Letting loose does not work for me.

And let's face it, what does Thom even know about responsibility? He's not a single parent. He's not a cancer survivor. He's not trying to figure out how to rebuild his life. It's all well and good for him to mansplain to me how I just need to ... whatever he thinks I should do. It's another thing to actually do what needs to get done.

So let's get this job done.

The first thing I pull out of the trunk of the Explorer is a fold-up dolly. It's my own personal one, because after doing a few events like this, I realized it would make hauling boxes so much easier.

And though I'm technically fully recovered, I still get nervous when I have to lift heavy things.

Thom's already off doing his DJ thing, greeting people and signing autographs.

I stack up three boxes—plastic ones that are clearly labeled now—and start to wheel toward the designated entrance.

"Look at this fancy deal. Where'd you get the wheels? Where did those bins come from? Don't we pitch everything in a big box at the end of the day? We like the chaos of not being able to find stuff and running out. It's fun being unprepared."

"That will never happen as long as I'm here. This is my job, and joke all you want, but I take it seriously. I know it's grunt work for pretty much minimum wage, but when I show up, I get the job done correctly."

I push past him, dragging the dolly behind me. Four trips in and out and I finally have all the stuff to begin setup, including a small air tank to blow up balloons for an archway and a large prize wheel.

By the time the tables and prizes are ready to go, I'm sweating like a stuffed pig. I pull the end of my large T-shirt out of my leggings and wipe my face. Is it hot in here or am I having yet another hot flash?

I may never know because before I have time to strip down so I don't melt, Thom is standing before me. "So yeah, Todd isn't going to make it. I'm going to need you to help me."

"What do you mean Todd isn't going to make it? Where is he?"

"He had some … car trouble."

"Can't he call an Uber? He needs to get here."

"Nah, we'll be fine without him."

"Who's this we? Do you have a mouse in your pocket or something?"

Thom leans in and whispers, "Margot, I need you to help me. Think of how it will look if you leave me hanging."

I clench my teeth—and maybe my fists as well. Dammit. He knows how to play me. He knows I can't say no.

"Oh, relax a little, will you? I was messing with you. In all honesty, you can say no. But it'll be fun. Think about how easy it was that day you were on the air. We'll banter a little and talk about the"—he looks around—"What charity again?"

"The American Red Cross. March is Red Cross Month. We're here to raise money and awareness for all they do, including but not limited to disaster relief, blood donation, and lifesaving training and certification."

Thom steps back and folds his arms over his chest. "See? A natural already."

"Can Todd get here? Maybe I can fill in for a little while. I don't know that I can do a full two hours. It's a lot of being on. I'm a more behind-the-scenes, organizational person."

"Todd isn't coming. So it's me, or it's us, and I think us could get a lot more money and attention."

"Are you sure? Maybe his car will be fine."

"Margot, Todd was in a car accident."

"Oh my God." My hands fly to my mouth. "Is he okay? What happened? Is he okay?"

Thom laughs. "You're repeating yourself. They think he fell asleep at the wheel. He's been dozing off a lot. I'm hoping the doctors admit him so they can figure out what's going on."

The concern on his face is evident. This is not a side of Thom I'm used to seeing.

I put my hand on his arm. "I'm sure they will."

"You didn't know Todd before, but something's not right. You know, my whole journey with UnBRCAble started because of Todd. I know he's got a lot of things going on, and he wouldn't take his health seriously. I started this, and started talking about it on the air, hoping that he'd take his health into his hands before it was too late. He doesn't do things that aren't his idea, so I thought if I planted the seed, maybe going to the doctor would become his idea."

Oh.

And I gave him nothing but crap for making me uncomfortable.

Well, now I have no choice but to help him out.

"Okay, but I don't really know what I'm doing."

"You can talk about the Red Cross and introduce the people we're supposed to interview. Maybe talk about the prizes a little. All the things that you set up."

He's got a point there. I talked with Meg Dyson no less than four times and emailed with her that many times a day about this event. I probably know these details more than Thom does. "Okay, sounds like a plan."

Thom gives me a small smile. It looks like he has a secret he's trying to keep from me.

"What's the Mona Lisa look for?"

He shakes his head. "I'll tell ya later."

CHAPTER 25

So I don't want to toot my own horn, but I'm sort of good at this.

Not sort of.

Meg said she had a goal of two thousand dollars while TJ the DJ and Todd were here. Even without half of the dynamic duo, we raised over three grand.

I am on top of the world.

See? Being organized and efficient isn't a bad thing. Mike, stick that in your pipe and smoke it.

The on-air bits weren't so bad either.

I'm fortunate that my music of choice is the 90s, so it fits in with the retro-Alternative programming of WBRC the Rock. Bailey often groans at my "old lady" choices in music, but it's serving me well. Though I keep hearing words like "classic" bandied about, which I refuse to accept.

I have to admit, today is a good day, Thom and all.

It's funny—when he's performing, whether it be on air or live, he is a different person than in private. It's like Thom is one person and TJ the DJ is another, and they just happen to live in the same body with the same horrible taste in shirts.

TJ the DJ is much more irreverent while Thom is more compassionate. There's a subtle difference, but I see it.

Anyway, as we wrap up the last ten minutes, I'm with TJ the DJ, so I go with it.

"One last spin on the wheel of chance!" I call out. The wheel is labeled with 90s band names, including the likes of Pearl Jam, Stone Temple Pilots, R.E.M., and Sublime.

"Okay, we've saved our best prize for last. Two VIP concert tickets to see Red Hot Chili Peppers, including backstage passes. A donation of fifty dollars or more will get you a spin. How do you win? Let's play living or dead. If you land on a band with a dead member, you're out. You've got to stay alive to win."

This sounds a little harsh, even for TJ. I add in to soften, "Just like the American Red Cross is there with lifesaving blood and CPR training and for your lifeguards. The Red Cross keeps you alive!"

TJ (as I'm now thinking of him in this setting) looks over at me and winks. "Okay, Vanna, are you ready for a spin?"

The prize wheel is surprisingly heavy to spin, and my arms are tired. I reach up and use all my strength to heave the wheel into motion. My arms flop down to my side as the lucky contestant watches anxiously.

I'm anxious too. I hope this guy wins so that I don't have to spin the wheel anymore.

It lands on Alice in Chains. He is not a winner.

I look at the wheel. In addition to Alice in Chains, there is Nirvana, Soundgarden, Sublime, Blind Melon, and Stone Temple Pilots that will necessitate another spin. The only winning slots are Pearl Jam and Red Hot Chili Peppers (naturally).

Dang, the 90s were rough on their lead singers.

The next contestant is up. Nirvana.

Blind Melon.

Crap.

Seriously, Thom is going to have to load this stuff up himself if I have to spin one more time.

I lean in and whisper, "I'm spent. We need a winner or else I won't be able to lift my arms again."

He leans in and whispers, "The more losers, the more money."

I roll my eyes. We've met our fundraising goal, and I'm ready to be done with this day. I've still got a full schedule ahead of me. Get Bailey to gymnastics. Cook dinner. Laundry. Always laundry. Pick Bailey up. Make sure homework is done. Clean up the kitchen.

When Frost said, "miles to go before I sleep," he could have been stating the case for every working mother out there.

One last spin. I can do this. This person has got to win. I throw everything I have into it. Here we go and *push*.

I step back, putting my hands on my hips to watch the wheel spin 'round and 'round. I'm sort of mesmerized by it, spacing out, when suddenly I feel arms clamp down around me.

Like a vice grip.

As I struggle against them, I feel my body being turned, and suddenly I'm squashed up against Thom's chest.

"What the hell?"

He does some weird turning thing, kicking his foot like he's dancing.

"What are you doing? Let go of me," I hiss through gritted teeth. "LET. ME. GO."

Thom looks out at the crowd. "Isn't it so exciting, Margot? Jeremy here won the VIP tickets and backstage passes to see Red Hot Chili Peppers next month!" He begins jumping up and down, still clutching me to his chest. I struggle against him, but he's freakishly—and quite deceptively—strong. He tilts his head so he's looking at the curtain backdrop.

"Seriously, Margot, trust me. Go with this."

"Let me go," I hiss again, trying to make my mouth look like a smile even though I want to stab Thom. Because when I break free and actually kill him, I don't want it to look premeditated.

"Margot, stop fighting and trust me."

"Why?"

"Trust me," he pleads.

Something in his voice makes me want to relax and melt into him, letting him protect and shelter me.

But then I remember that no one in my life has ever done that for me, and this virtual stranger has no reason to protect me.

I push back, leaning away.

Thom shakes his head and says, "I tried to help you, but you have to let me."

"Hey, Mommy, look! A prize fell out of that lady's shirt!" a small voice calls out.

Thom looks down at his feet. I follow his gaze to see what he's looking at.

It's not that big. Maybe the size of a deck of cards. Except it's not a deck of cards. It's a flesh-colored, triangle-shaped pillow.

Exactly like the one I put inside my bra to make me look like I have boobs.

My hands fly to my chest where, to my horror, my right side is suspiciously flat.

My prosthetic boob insert has fallen out.

In public.

Not only in public, but in front of at least a hundred people. And a TV crew filming for the evening news.

My hands covering my chest as if I were topless, I bend down to grab the escapee. But I do so too quickly, losing my balance. I crash into the prize wheel, which topples over into the curtain backdrop.

There is shrieking and screaming as people start running. Someone steps on me, forcing me flat on my back, splayed out across a scene of wreckage and destruction.

But still holding my bra stuffing in my hand for the six o'clock news—and the world—to see.

I look up to see the crowd staring, a mix of concern and laughter on their faces. Great. I'm now officially a laughingstock.

Hot tears burn my eyes as I struggle to get up. The setup is in shambles, yet it's still markedly better than my pride. Thom's there, pulling me to my feet.

I pick up my wayward insert and stuff it into the waistband of my pants.

"You okay?"

I shake my head, unable to form words to express how mortified I am.

"Oh my God, Marg, I thought that was you! What happened?"

I close my eyes, willing the voice to go away. Yet when I open my eyes, Sandy Beemer, my former PTO arch-nemesis, is still standing there.

Because, of course, Sandy Beemer had to witness this.

The only thing that would have made it any more embarrassing is if Mike saw too.

Thom gently turns me away from Sandy. "She's fine."

I can defend myself. I turn back. "Yeah, you know, clumsy me. I was starting to take the display down and something stuck, and whoops. But as long as you've stopped by to show you care, Sandy, would you consider extending that caring by donating to the American Red Cross? I know you know how much lifesaving work they do. Oh, and there's a sign-up for their next blood drive too."

Sandy pales slightly. "I don't like needles. Sorry," she says, wrinkling her nose.

"Right, I get it. I don't like them either. But I received transfusions during my mastectomy and follow-up surgeries, so now I understand the importance. Here's a flyer"—I pick one up off the ground—"Thanks for stopping by."

Sandy takes it, turning quickly away. I start to clean up.

I want to die. I want to die. I want to die.

Instead of curling into a fetal position and weeping, I clean. I pick up and put into boxes. I right the background. I fetch the scattered flyers. I push down the tears and the mortification.

This is why my life is such a mess. Because I am. And I'm not sure which is worse—my prosthetic falling out or me falling over.

Equally humiliating.

I'm going to have to quit this job. That is, if they don't fire me first.

Oh yes, Jack will absolutely fire me. No doubt about it.

I don't say a word as I pack up and take loads of boxes out to the car. When people try to talk to me, I shrug them off, letting my hair fall in front of my face to block the world out.

Thom is busy chatting with people, both fans and the Red Cross staff. Seeing him in full TJ the DJ mode is somewhat impressive. He's simultaneously irreverent and engaging. Like that comic who says those things you can't believe he actually said yet laugh at the same time.

I'm grateful he's taking the attention away from me.

I take the last of the stuff out to the Explorer and get in the vehicle. It's only then, in the quiet of the SUV, that I allow a few tears to slip out. How is this my life?

Everything I've worked so hard for, so carefully planned for, has been reduced to me in a pile on the floor at the mall with a half-empty bra.

There's a soft knock on the window. Thom gives me a small wave and motions for me to roll down the window.

Totally aside, but do kids today even know what that gesture means? Technology, like power windows, has them missing out on so much.

"Yes?"

"Slide over. I'll drive back to the station."

"No, it's okay."

"You're upset. I can drive."

"I can multitask being upset and driving. After all, I'm a mother. I've had sixteen years of practice. Now get in."

He walks around to the passenger side and slides in. "Are you sure?"

"As you so politely reminded me at the onset of this excursion, this is my job. I might be a failure at everything I attempt, but I take my responsibilities seriously. This is my job right now, and I'm going to do it."

I can feel him staring at me as I pull onto the street. A quick glance confirms it. I return my gaze to the road and focus on that, staring straight ahead.

After a few minutes, I can't take it any longer. "What?" I snap.

"You."

I roll my eyes. "Yes, I know. I'm a disaster. I'm mortifying and clumsy and am probably getting fired as soon as we pull into the parking lot."

"Fired?"

Thom actually has the audacity to sound perplexed.

"Yes, I'm sure as soon as Jack hears—or sees—what happened, he'll fire me. He's been looking for the excuse, and I handed it to him on a silver platter."

"What are you talking about?"

"Jack hates me."

"Jack is totally intimidated by you. He's in awe of everything you do. I think he's a little starstruck. Or he has a crush on you. Or both."

I look over at Thom, swerving the wheel of the Explorer as I do.

"Whoa there, speedy. Keep your eyes on the road before you kill us. Todd was already in an accident today. We can't take both of us out of commission in one day."

"Sorry. Sorry," I mutter. "What do you mean?"

Thom laughs. "You honestly don't have a clue, do you? I thought it was all an act, but it's not. You really don't know. You really don't see it."

"Know what? See what? What act?"

"You're good at everything. And even when you're not, you're so damn competent that you figure it out on the fly. I've never met someone who has their shit together as much as you do."

It's a good thing I'm pulling into the parking lot because I don't think I can keep driving with this revelation.

"What do you mean?" I wail. "My shit is not together. It's in a big flaming heap and literally falling out of my shirt on the evening news!"

And with that, Thom bursts out laughing.

"You see? You have a sense of humor about these things."

I wasn't saying it to be funny, but it's hard not to laugh at the absurdity of it all. It's either laugh or cry, and I'll be damned if I let him see me cry.

"Get out of the car," Thom says abruptly. He changes the directions of his thoughts so often I could probably collect workers' comp for whiplash.

I'm too spent to do anything but obey. Thom walks around the front of the car to me and opens his arms.

"What are you doing?"

"Giving you a much-needed hug." And with that, his arms close in around me.

There's a silence that's not as awkward as it should be. Well, that is until Thom says, "I bet you don't get hugged very often."

That's all it takes. I fall apart like a cheap suit.

Dammit.

CHAPTER 26

Instantly, I'm a mess. Clinging, sobbing, snotting.

All the things I saw my mom do every time a man told her he was leaving. All the things I promised myself I'd never do.

I didn't even do this when Mike left.

Well, not that he could see.

In between the sobs, I gasp out, "I ... just ... want ... to ... be ... perfect."

I feel Thom's body shaking a little under mine, so I pull back. He's laughing.

"Are you laughing at me?" Angrily I wipe the tears from my face. He makes me be vulnerable, and then he laughs at me?

This is what I get for letting him see the real me.

His arms are still around my waist. "No, I'm not laughing at you. I'm laughing at the idea that you are striving for perfection and that you're this hard on yourself for not achieving it. Haven't you heard? Nobody's perfect."

"Well, I know that, but I have to be as close to it as I can. I try so hard."

"No one would ever doubt that."

"Then why am I such a failure? Why am I never good enough?"

"Good enough for what?"

I notice for the first time that Thom's light brown eyes are the exact color I take my coffee. They are also kind eyes, full of compassion and bookended by wrinkles from years of laughter.

"Good enough to be loved." My voice comes out a hoarse whisper. "I try so hard, and people still hate me."

Thom brushes a strand of hair off my face, much like I used to do to Bailey when she was upset about something. She won't let me within ten feet of her these days, even if a tag is sticking out or her hair is sticking up. "No one hates you."

"My kids do. My ex does. Jack does."

"Teenagers are raging assholes, so don't take it personally. Your ex is the world's biggest douche canoe, so don't take it personally. And Jack does not hate you. I think he's in love with you."

"What?" I know Thom just said this, but it still doesn't make sense to me.

"At least a platonic, awestruck kind of love. We've had all sorts of celebrities and rock stars in, and he's never been as tongue-tied as he is around you. The way you came in and set him straight in the interview—"

"He *told* you about that?" My hands cover my face. "I plead the fifth. I plead insanity. I plead inconsistent hormones and early menopause. I—"

Thom pulls my hands away from my face. "Don't you understand that you are exactly what the station needs? What Jack needs? Jack is people savvy, which is why he deals with the talent and guests so well. However, he's not great on the business end, which is why Liberty Media and WBRC is in trouble. Was in trouble. Since you came on board and started organizing and streamlining, things are looking up."

"But I'm just an office grunt. I mean, I spent weeks organizing the swag room and the back room."

"And do you know how much money that has saved the station? Our swag and prize budget was through the roof. By knowing what we have and using it appropriately, we've dropped spending by twenty percent. Trust me, you're going far with Liberty Media. If I were you, I'd be asking for a raise."

"I just made a colossal ass out of myself on the news."

Thom shrugs. "Accidents happen. No one's going to blame you for falling. It's not like you were drunk or high, which is usually the case when something like that happens at the radio station."

I shake my head. How can he be so cavalier about all this?

"Plus, it'll get us publicity, which is the whole point in us being out in the community."

"And to help out the American Red Cross."

"That too." He laughs. "Obviously, we're only out to be do-gooders and do good of the goodly sort."

Now I'm laughing. "You have a gift for the English language."

"Thanks. I went to school for writing. I'm glad to see it hasn't been wasted."

"Writing?" We're still standing in the parking lot of Liberty Media, in front of the Explorer. Even with my jacket, and now that I'm no longer in Thom's arms, I'm getting cold. I tuck my hands under my arms to keep them warm.

"It's a long story for another day. I need to get moving. See you in the morning?"

I look down, sad at the thought of going home to wallow in my humiliation alone. But it's my life, and I need to get used to it.

"Yup, sure thing." I turn and walk toward my car. I'm supposed to unpack the station vehicle and bring everything inside, but frankly, I'm too tired. It'll wait until I get here in the morning. In fact, I'll come in early so I can take care of it before my work shift starts.

Though Thom tried to make me feel better by saying that about Jack, I know it's a load of bull. It has to be. I've done nothing but yell and make an ass out of myself during my time at Liberty Media. I don't know how anyone could like that.

I pull into my garage, and I'm barely in the house before Bailey is standing before me, hands on her hips. "Mom." Her tone is grave.

I'm in for it.

"Bailey, I've had a long day. Is your homework done? I've got to get you to gymnastics."

"*Mom*."

I sigh. "What?"

"How could you? It's all over the news. You're a laughingstock. It's going to go viral."

I close my eyes and wish the floor could swallow me whole. It's like every taunt and torment I suffered through in my childhood is now echoing through my brain.

"Did you even think about that? What are people going to say? I'm never going to be able to show my face at school again."

Somewhere in the back of my head, I know Bailey is only thirteen, and her hormones are raging, and everything feels so big. I do know that. But in this moment, I understand so deeply what she's feeling. And that she's focusing on all the wrong things. It shouldn't matter what others think. It should matter how *I'm* feeling.

"I'm pretty sure I had no way of controlling falling over. It's called losing your balance. You should know. You do it all the time at gymnastics. I don't yell at you for embarrassing me, do I? No, I'm pretty sure I make sure you're okay and encourage you to get up and try again."

Her mouth tightens. "But, Mom, the *other thing*." She gestures to my chest.

Oh yes, she saw that.

And it's in that moment that I know what the right decision for me is. I reach inside and pull out the prosthetics that fill my bra. "You mean this? Don't worry. It won't happen again."

"Ugh, Mom, put those away. I can't believe you stuff your bra. Kadence did that last year, but I thought you were better."

I start to tell her that I'm not the same as a desperate preteen, wanting to fit a mold for people to like me, but then I realize I'm exactly like that.

"Yes, well, it's hard when society constantly rams a message down our throats of what we are supposed to look like. And be like. And it's really hard when the outside, and inside for that matter, don't match these things."

Bailey doesn't say anything, so I take that as encouragement to go on. "I never talked a lot about my health with you and Jordan because I didn't want to worry you. I grew up in a home that was uncertain, and I worried all the time. I wanted better for you and your brother. I don't know what you remember about the end of first grade, but during that time, I had a lump in my breast."

"Ugh, Mom, that's gross."

"Listen, I know no one wants to hear about their parents' private parts, but this could affect you too. Actually, believe it or not, it could affect Jordan too."

"Mom, boys don't have boobs." She rolls her eyes.

I call for Jordan, and he comes in, shuffling his feet. I motion for him to remove his earbuds, which he does with a sigh. I start the story over for him.

"... It was precancerous. Then I found another about a year later. That one was cancerous. They did some testing and found out that I have a genetic mutation that makes it really likely I'll get breast or ovarian cancer. And since I already had breast cancer, I wasn't taking any more chances. Six years ago, I had a preventative salpingo-oophorectomy and hysterectomy and then a mastectomy."

"Yeah, I remember that. Gam came to stay for a while," Jordan pipes up. "You didn't look sick, so I couldn't figure out why you had operations."

"I remember Gam being here." Bailey wrinkles her nose. "So your boobs are fake? Gross. Then why are you stuffing your bra?" She punctuates the sentence with a gagging noise.

Jordan rolls his eyes.

"Well, the surgery I had at Christmas time was to take those implants out. There was a recall on them, and they were making me sick. They made my body reject them. It's why I was tired and always had headaches and diarrhea. I needed to have them taken out."

"That's what you were doing? Dad said you were having a nip and a tuck. I thought that meant like liposuction or something," Bailey says.

"Yeah, and I thought it was a really bad time to do something you didn't need to have done. I thought that's why Dad left, because you were more concerned about how you looked than us," Jordan adds.

My heart shatters. "Guys, you know me better. Would I ever be *more* concerned with how I looked than you guys?"

"How you look is very important to you," Bailey says with a nod.

Their words hurt. The fact that they don't think I love them more than anything means I've failed them.

"How I look will never be more important than the two of you."

"Yeah, Mom. We know that. But you are into how things look to everyone else. Things don't have to be perfect all the time, you know. It's okay to make some mistakes or not have a vacuumed rug or perfect hair all the time."

Jordan's making some good points, and I feel a tiny bit of relief that he knows how much I love them.

"I know, and I know that sometimes I do focus too much on how things look. It's ... hard. I had a difficult time growing up. My dad left when I was little, and I always thought that if I had been prettier or better behaved, maybe he would have stayed."

"Mom, that's stupid." Leave it to my brash thirteen-year-old to set me straight. "Your dad didn't leave because of you or Uncle Arlo, just like Dad didn't leave because of me or Jordan."

I'm glad she won't carry the burden of guilt with her as I have all these years. A weight lifts slightly.

"He left because of you. It's your fault."

And now the weight comes crashing back.

But I don't want to accept it. It shouldn't be all on me. There were two of us in this marriage. I'm not the one who gave up. My kids need a lesson about responsibility.

"Can you explain why it's my fault?" I keep my tone in check so neither kid can see how upset I really am that they think this is all on me.

Jordan starts. "Well, you know, you always have to have things your way."

"Like ..." I prompt.

"You want the house picked up and counters wiped off and the floors vacuumed and the dishes done. Like, every day."

"Right. And who does that?"

"You do."

I nod. "So I want the house clean and orderly, and I do all the work. Yes, that's a hard way to live. What else?"

It's Bailey's turn. "You want us to get good grades and make us do homework."

"Yes, because you need to take pride in and responsibility for your own work so you can live up to your potential and be your best selves. What else?"

Jordan again. "You're always volunteering and doing good. You never say no, and you want people to like you."

I nod. "Yes, I believe service is a virtue that we all should possess, and I want to teach you guys by example. Plus, most of my volunteering is for you two. So that you could have class parties and field trips and treats at school. So that the swim team could buy those team jackets and the gymnastics team could travel for meets and so that everyone could be included, especially those kids whose parents couldn't afford to do those things."

Both kids look at me.

"And as for my relationship with your father, I took my marriage vows seriously. In sickness and in health.

Forsaking all others. I made a comfortable—yes, clean—home for him. It's what he wanted and expected. I cooked his food and washed his clothes and raised his children. I listened to his problems and supported him through tough times. I tried to be everything he could want in a partner. But you know, I still really can't see how him getting a girlfriend and leaving me is my fault. Perhaps we'll have to agree to disagree on this one."

I'm done with defending myself. I stand up and retreat to my room.

I've had enough of this day.

CHAPTER 27

The kids are on their own to take the bus today. I've got to get into work to unpack from yesterday's epic failure.

It's not like me to leave something unfinished.

My whole life right now is not like me.

Especially the *thing* I've been thinking about all night.

I need to talk to someone about it. I know what I'll be bringing up at tonight's UnBRCAble meeting. Let's hope I can keep myself together and not lose it on Thom before I get to talk about this.

I don't know why he brings it out in me. In all honesty, he's been nothing but kind. He may appear to be insensitive, and there's a distinct lack of separation between what he says on air and the people in his personal life, but he's been a good ... friend.

And I have not.

I take a detour into Cider Belly Doughnuts, picking up a dozen for him. I've never met a person who cannot be bought off with these delicious confections. I add in a large coffee, light and sweet, which is how Thom takes it.

I'm surprised I know even that detail about him. I've not been reciprocating in the listening department. I bet frequent listeners of the show know more about him than I do.

If I'd acted this way toward Mike, I'd say it was no wonder he left me. Yet Thom doesn't run away.

I don't understand him. Hell, I don't understand Mike either. I'm not even sure I understand myself.

Still, this will be a good start to turning over a new leaf. That's what I have to do. I'm a little behind the eight ball with my new journey, but I can catch up. The new Marg will take a little more time to listen to others before bulldozing her way through, making sure everything is just so.

I pull into the parking lot, feeling good about my decision to be more of a giver and more of a listener. To reciprocate what Thom's done for me. I'll get the car unloaded and then bring in the coffee and doughnuts for him.

But as I approach the Explorer, my heart sinks into my stomach. It's empty. All the boxes, the tables, everything is all gone. I left them in the Explorer, and they were stolen. Hundreds of dollars' worth of merchandise and gift cards, not to mention the sound system, which had to be worth multiple thousands of dollars.

I think I'm going to vomit.

All because I was too tired and too embarrassed to get the job done. Jack isn't even going to have to fire me. I'm going to quit on grounds of my own incompetence.

Just when I think I can't screw things up anymore, I find a way to top myself.

I can't afford to replace this stuff. I'm going to have to work for years to pay it back. I won't be able to afford my mortgage. We're going to be homeless and destitute all because my boob fell out on local TV.

I watched it over and over last night. There it was, my fake boob pillow dropping out of my shirt. Then, as I turn, you can clearly see that my left side is flat while my right side is not.

You can also see that Thom was trying to cover it up, and I was fighting him tooth and nail.

These doughnuts, no matter how good they are, are not going to be enough.

Maybe if I'd bought Jack some too, he'd forget that I'm a disaster.

I square my shoulders. Time to face the music.

No pun intended.

As I walk into Liberty Media for the last time, I carefully balance the coffee and doughnuts. Hopefully, it'll soften the bad news I'm about to deliver.

As it's only seven, no one is here yet besides Thom, Todd, and Smudge the Producer. Great. I get to wait for Jack to arrive so I can tell him.

Quietly, I enter the booth. Smudge smiles at me, and Thom waves me in, pulling the lollipop stick out of his mouth. Todd's seat is empty.

As stealthily as I can while carrying my goods, I creep into the inner booth. Thom tilts his head, indicating I should sit in Todd's seat. I do, easing the doughnuts onto the table and sliding the coffee over to Thom.

"Alright, peeps. We've got a special guest in the studio with us today. Lady K, slide those headphones on and flip that red switch on your mic. Smudge the Producer, make sure Lady K is live."

Just like that, I'm on the air again.

Mental note: never come into the booth when Thom is on the air.

"Um, hi."

"Hi yourself. So, Lady K finds herself a bit of a celebrity this morning due to an incident that occurred during our live appearance yesterday."

I want to crawl under the table and never come out.

"I can't believe you brought that up. I don't want to talk about it."

"But it's important that you do."

"Okay, let's get this out of the way. I know you're all going to Google it anyway as soon as I'm done. I'm a breast cancer survivor, diagnosed in my mid-thirties, and I had a mastectomy and reconstruction. I've had some complications from my surgeries, and my implants were recalled, so I'm in between reconstructions at the time being. So yes, I wear prosthetic breast fillers to give me the silhouette I'm used to having. And yes, one fell out. In public. On the news. So that's what happened, and now can me move on? Oh, and I fell over too, trying to get my prosthetic before the world saw it. Okay, that's it. End of story. I don't want to talk about it again. Moving on."

I'm done talking, and I'm not going to say anything else.

Thom looks at me for a beat and then like nothing has happened says, "Lady K has arrived bearing gifts in the form of coffee and doughnuts from Cider Belly. I've never had these before."

That's all it takes to break me out of my resolve to be silent.

"You've never had Cider Belly before? Then I'm glad I'm here to right a wrong."

"Who are you? Dr. Sam Beckett from *Quantum Leap*?"

"Oh, remember that show? I had a little crush on Scott Bakula. I found it on TV recently and tried showing it to my kids. They laughed at the technology. Computers were such a new idea back then." I look over at Thom, who is smiling. "Maybe I am Dr. Sam Beckett and you're Al, wearing that"—I catch myself before I stay stupid—"Hawaiian shirt. Seriously, why do you always wear those shirts? I've never seen you in anything but. Do you even sleep in them?"

This question has taken up more of my mental space than I care to admit since the day Thom first walked into UnBRCAble.

"It started when I was in college. I'd gone to a beach party the night before and despite my best intentions to have a low-key evening, I was out a lot later than expected. I had to interview the dean for the college TV station at eight a.m., so I showed up as was, complete with a thrift store Hawaiian shirt. The dean was visibly irritated, and the interview became something of a campus sensation. The faculty advisor that ran the TV studio fired me, and the radio station snatched me up. That manager said it didn't matter what I wore because it was radio."

"I guess better to have a wardrobe that belongs in radio than a face," I quip.

"Right? I immediately became known as Tahiti TJ. Fans used to send me shirts. I haven't bought one for myself in about ten years. I have to have at least a hundred."

"I don't think I've ever seen you wear the same one twice. I didn't know there were that many different prints in the world. Do you even own a normal shirt?"

Thom winks at me. "What is normal anyway?"

"You know, normal. Like me."

Thom laughs. "Right, Lady K. I don't think we need to discuss how normal you are. Or aren't. Do we want to get into it?"

"Shouldn't we play a song or something? The listeners don't want us yammering. They want their music. Push your button and put some tunes on."

"Aye-aye, Captain." With a few clicks on his computer, Candlebox instantly fills the studio. Thom lowers the volume.

"I can't believe you brought that up," I hiss.

"I had to. Had to get it out of the way. You know, you could be a great voice for women going through this."

"I don't want to be a voice. I want never to speak of it again. Capisce?"

Thom smiles. "Are you even Italian?"

"No, but I play one on TV."

Thom shakes his head, laughing. "I'm glad you stopped in when you did. Todd isn't back yet, and I need a co-host for the morning."

"Can't you do it alone?"

"Like other things, you certainly can do it alone, but it's much more fun with another person."

I blush at his innuendo, as immediately a totally inappropriate thought flashes through my brain.

Whoa. Where did *that* come from?

"Is Todd okay?" I manage to croak out. God, if he only knew where my mind went, he'd never let me live it down. Or he'd run screaming.

Or both.

"Eh, who knows? I think he's diabetic, which isn't hard to guess looking at his physique. I should probably eat his share of these doughnuts to protect him. To what do I owe this treat?"

The thrill of being on the radio subsides as I remember not only my mortification yesterday, but then the ramifications of my colossal screwup by leaving all the stuff in the car to be stolen.

"Yeah, well, they were meant as a thank you for dealing with the hot mess that is me but consider them a good-bye as well."

"Good-bye? I don't understand."

"Yeah, as soon as Jack gets in, he's going to fire me."

Thom sighs and rolls his eyes. "This line is getting tired. He doesn't hate you." He clicks his mouse, and the next song starts.

"Yeah, but this time I messed up big-time. I was so upset last evening that I didn't unpack the car. I came in early to get it done, so it didn't take away from my assigned work time. But the Explorer's empty. Someone stole all the stuff." I put my head down on the table. "All the swag and prizes. The gift cards. The sound system. Jack can't ignore this. It's going to cost the station lots. I can't afford to pay it back. I can barely afford my mortgage."

The sound-canceling headset is gently being pulled away from my ears. "Margot, what are you talking about?"

I sit up. "I left everything in the car, and now it's all gone. He has to fire me for this. It would be irresponsible of him not to."

"Margot," he drawls, saying my full name as he always does. "I unpacked the Explorer. I did it when I got here this morning."

"But … how? Why? What time did you get up?"

"I didn't sleep well, so I figured instead of tossing and turning, I might as well make myself useful. I should have helped you with it yesterday. I'm sorry I was busy doing the DJ schmoozing thing. That stuff was heavy."

I'm glad he says this. I thought I was just being a wimp about it.

"But … how? Why?" I repeat. My brain is having a difficult time processing his kindness and generosity, especially when I have not always reciprocated.

"You sound like a broken record." He turns to his computer for a second. "Oh crap, dead air." With the click of a mouse, Thom leans back into the mic, simultaneously sliding his headphones back into place.

"Sorry about that, good listeners. I'm here with my special, in-studio guest, Lady K."

I also adjust my headphones. "Sorry to be distracting you, TJ the DJ." That name sounds foreign on my tongue. "TJ just told me I sounded like a broken record. I bet my kids don't even know what that means."

"I started in the days of CDs before digital took over. It's so much easier now. Digital never skips."

"Right? But when you had an album, be it vinyl or CD, that skipped, you will forever anticipate hearing that skip whenever you hear the song. When I play Dave Matthews Band, "Two Step" on Alexa, I wait for the skip. She doesn't know it's supposed to be there."

"For me, it was the mixed tapes that I made, and the tape would run out mid song. Then I always debated if I started the song over on the other side or lived life unfulfilled."

"YES!" I say a little too enthusiastically. "Sorry, I'm learning volume control," I apologize as I see Smudge the Producer frantically waving at me to keep my voice down. "Oh, kids don't know about mixed tapes either. I spent the better part of the summer of 1988 glued to my pink radio/cassette recorder, trying to get my favorite songs so I could make up dances to them."

"Who were your favorites?"

I have to think, channeling back to my thirteen-year-old self. "Debbie Gibson, Richard Marx, Gloria

Estefan, and of course, Whitney Houston. How about you?"

"I was sixteen that summer, so I thought I was all cool listening to Poison and Def Leppard."

"Oh my God. You had long hair, didn't you?"

"Yes, and that was the summer I started smoking too. Man, I was an idiot."

"You're a smoker? I've never smelled it on you." I think about when he held me yesterday and that first time he gave me a ride in his car. I couldn't predict where this conversation is going if I'd had a map right in front of me. I sniff in his general direction. "You don't still smoke, do you? I can't smell it."

He picks up a new lollipop from a bowl next to him and sticks it in his mouth. "Gave it up last year. Had to. When you find out you are probably going to get cancer of some kind, you don't want to give it any better of a chance than it already has. Okay, so for you, Lady K, without the skips, here's the Dave Matthews Band."

He slides his headset back so one ear is exposed.

"That was fun. You're a natural."

"Is my mic off?" I whisper.

"Yes," Thom whispers back, "and if it weren't, everyone would hear you say that because you're talking right into it."

Right.

I lean back and expose my ear.

"So the lollipop thing is because of smoking?"

"Made sense to quit. I don't have many vices in life. Smoking was about it. But yeah, I started doing the lollipops when I was trying to quit, and now that's my vice."

I sit back, folding my arms across my chest. Normally I do this because I'm self-conscious and trying to hide myself. Today, I do it in a contemplative manner. "You are one interesting character, aren't you?"

Thom mimics my pose. "I could say the same thing about you."

And then I smile at him.

CHAPTER 28

"So you're, like, a DJ now?" Becky laughs. "I so did *not* see this one coming."

"Make that two of us, and I'm just filling in while Todd is recovering. Hopefully, he'll be back next week."

"But you and TJ the DJ are so cute together. Totally adorbs."

"Don't say 'adorbs.' You're in your mid-forties, not fourteen."

"I don't think fourteen-year-olds say it either, but any way you slice it, you guys are totally cute. I'm going to ship you so hard."

"Again, mid-forties, not fourteen. I don't need to be shipped. I'm not doing relationships anyway. I mean, seriously, how can I? Not to mention, it's not like that. Thom is a friend."

Yeah, a friend that maybe I had a dream about once. Or twice.

I can't even remember the last time I had a dream like that. I'm not sure if I've even had one since my hysterectomy.

I certainly can't remember the last time I had those thoughts about my own husband. Ex-husband, I should say.

Mike was so hungry for freedom that he gave me everything I asked for in the divorce settlement, including speed and outright ownership of the house. He's also seeing the kids regularly, which they need.

It doesn't bother me, though I know on some level I should be distraught. These past four months without Mike have shown me that maybe I wasn't really happy with him. I didn't realize how exhausting it was trying to please him all the time. Afraid that if I wasn't perfect, he'd leave.

I guess that was a self-fulfilling prophecy.

But honestly, I don't think I could have done more.

And here I am, a few short months later, thinking things I shouldn't be about my co-worker.

"Beck, it's not like I could even contemplate a relationship. A. Thom hasn't indicated any interest. B. I'm not sure I'm interested. And C. the boob situation. As in, I haven't got any."

"Well, I talked to Doug about that."

"You were talking to your husband about my boobs?"

"I talk to you about his crooked penis and his hemorrhoids, so yes, I talked to him about your boobs. I asked him if we should postpone our road trip this summer so I can help you out."

I have to sit down. "Becky, no. I can't ask you to do that. I won't ask you to. It's not that important."

"Your breasts? Your womanhood is not that important? I'd say it's a lot more important than some stupid trip."

"It's not a stupid trip. It's your family. Your kids will tell their kids who will tell their kids. It's their legacy. It's time you'll never have again. I already don't have breasts. It's not going to kill me. I'm no less of a woman without them."

As I'm vehemently refusing my best friend's help, once I end the call, I realize I've come to a decision.

I am no less of a woman without them.

I think.

Maybe.

No, I can't do that.

Or can I?

Okay, so maybe I haven't come to a decision, other than I can't let my best friend give up the trip she's been planning for years. Even if I were on my deathbed, I'd want her to go.

Lucky for me, I'm not on my deathbed. My cancer was caught super early. I had access to cancer-suppressing drugs. And I had the possibly mutant tissues removed from my body.

So what that I look like I've been hit with shrapnel and stitched back together in the field? I'm here, still standing. Still kicking ass and taking names.

Whoa.

Where did this newfound courage and bravado come from?

This is so not me.

Crippling self-doubt and second-guessing? That's me.

A pathological desire to please? *C'est moi.*

Confidence?

I am not familiar with this concept.

It's unsettling.

I'm not sure I like it.

Somehow, I feel as if Thom would understand.

He puts himself out there all the time, and he doesn't seem to care. I wish I could go through life not caring. How does he do it?

I walk into my bathroom, trying to process the idea running through my head. Could I really do it?

I pull my shirt over my head and toss it onto the floor. Next comes the bra and the prosthetics. I stand in front of my mirror and look.

To be sure, it's not pretty.

Before my mastectomy, nursing my two babies had taken its toll on my body. My breasts were no longer pretty and perky, and I didn't mind because they had nourished my children.

Flourished my children.

For that alone, I am grateful.

Even after my breasts were carefully crafted and were, dare I say, perfect, it wasn't enough for my husband.

I wasn't enough for my husband.

In reality, he wasn't enough for me.

If he had been, maybe I wouldn't have been so insecure.

I cup the sagging skin, pulling it to the side, trying to imagine what I would look like without anything there. I turn to the side, gauging what a totally flat profile would look like.

If I were still with Mike, I'd never even consider this.

But I'm not, and so I am thinking about it.

Going flat.

Staying flat.

No more implants. No more reconstruction. No more prosthetics.

No more cleavage. No more nipples. No more bras.

No more surgeries.

No more perfection.

The gravity of that thought sends chills of fear down my spine. How will anyone love me if I'm not perfect?

My phone dings, breaking me out of my spiraling thoughts.

Thank God.

It's a message that my cell phone payment has posted. Hard to read something deep into that, but it still provides the break I need. Quickly, I slip my sports bra back on, followed by my shirt.

I pick up my phone and dial without thinking. "Are you busy?"

"Come on over." No other words. Nothing else needed. Three words. Relief floods me.

I rush to my car before I realize I don't know where Thom lives. A moment later, an address pops up in my text messages.

Seven minutes later, I ring the doorbell.

"Are you okay?" Thom asks as I walk through the door.

"I need help. I don't know what to do. I'm thinking about something, and I don't know if I should do it. I don't know if I *can* do it."

The first thing I notice is Thom's shirt: a bevy of repeating toucans. Next, I take in his living room. Clean lines with retro mid-century modern furnishings. Framed album covers collage the wall above the white brick fireplace.

I can analyze his style choices later. I need to tell him what I'm contemplating.

The decision to live without breasts.

"I think you need to do what is right for you. And nobody else but you."

"But how will someone love me if I look like that? Men don't want damaged goods. It's why I try so hard to be perfect."

Thom holds his hands up. "Wait. What did you just say?"

"Damaged goods? Obviously, I'm quite damaged. Both emotionally and physically. I always thought if I could work hard enough, I could erase those scars."

"You don't erase scars. You heal them."

"No, I want to erase them. Like they were never there."

"Then it's no wonder you're not happy. It's no wonder your marriage didn't work out. You're going about this all wrong."

"Excuse me?"

"You're totally wrong with this. Look at your body. You have scars, and your scars are beautiful."

"I'll be even more scarred."

"You have to do what's right for you. What feels right in this moment. No one can choose this for you, and it's totally your choice. Not what you think someone wants for you. What you want for you."

"I want to be loved. Absolutely and unconditionally." It has nothing to do with my breasts.

"Then I think you need to start giving that gift to yourself."

CHAPTER 29

"Are you sure?" Dr. Chung asks.

"Of course I'm not sure. I wanted to talk about it." Sometimes I think Dr. Chung is more like my therapist than my surgeon. "This wasn't something I'd ever considered before, but now I am. So tell me the deets. What's it mean to go flat?"

"I'd carefully remove your excess breast skin and nipples. You'd have horizontal scars here." He draws a line with his finger, right about where a perky breast nipple should be. "Though depending on how things go, the scars may have a bit of a curve to them, or there may be even two lines going *here* and *here*."

I'm too impatient for him to finish, so I jump in. "I want an aesthetic skin closure." I've been doing my research. Still, Google is no substitute for talking to an actual health professional. But at least I know the questions to ask.

"Yes, of course. I know you, Marg, and I know you have looked into this. An aesthetic skin closure does not leave the possibility for reconstruction at a later date. It's the final surgery. I will leave you with a smooth contour. You will not have any puckering or skin flaps at the lateral edge. It will look a million times better than what you currently have."

Well, duh. Anything would look better.

"I've read a lot about women who wanted to go flat but were left with deformities. I've had enough of that."

"You know me better than that. Why now?"

I take a deep breath. "Mike left me." I don't want to get into the details, but I feel as if Dr. Chung needs to know. As if knowing will make him do a better job for me in my surgery. "He was cheating on me, and I found out when I was in the hospital the last time. I always wanted to look good, for him. I thought if I was pretty enough and slim enough and perfect enough, he'd never leave me. Well, fat lot of good that did me."

"Listen, if he cheated on you, that says something about him and not about you."

"I'm starting to realize that. And we both know reconstruction with implants probably isn't a good idea. Because of the stress in my life, I'm having trouble gaining enough weight to have a DIEP flap reconstruction. Also, now that I'm single, I can't take the time off work or away from my kids to heal from that surgery. I can't afford it either. "

I take a deep breath before I say the last thing. "And when you have your prosthetic boob fall out on TV, you start to wonder why the hell are you even bothering?"

Dr. Chung winces. He saw the video. Great.

"So here's what I want to know: if I decide to go through with an aesthetic flat closure, how will you prevent dog ears? What about concavity? I don't mind if I'm flat, but I don't want them making craters on my chest. Will you have one incision or multiple? Do you sit me up during surgery to see what effect gravity is having?"

I'm sort of impressed with myself for remembering all those questions without writing them down. During the height of my breast implant illness–induced fog, I couldn't even keep track of when my appointments were, let alone a list of things to ask the doctor.

After Dr. Chung answers my questions in detail, he smiles. "I never saw you as one to go this route, but if and when you're ready, I'm here and I've got you."

I leave his office also smiling. My chest, in its current state, is hideous and deformed. But it doesn't always have to be.

Cancer, and my genetic predisposition toward it, already took my breasts. It's time for me to reclaim my self-confidence.

That bravado lasts until I arrive home to Mike's car in my driveway. Our divorce was final last week. What the hell is he doing here?

"What are you doing here?" As part of the divorce settlement, Mike signed the house over to me without forcing me to buy him out. I want to scream at him that he's on my property, and I'll have him arrested for trespassing.

That would be awesome.

Except it would hurt my kids, so I won't. Also, I don't want to look like a vindictive B, even though I very much am.

"You're on the radio now?"

I shrug. "Sometimes. What's it to you?"

"Who came up with that brilliant plan?"

I stand and fold my arms over my lumpy, saggy breast sacks. I bet it will feel a lot better when I'm flat.

When I'm flat.

It sounds like a hopeful thing.

"The good people at Liberty Media value my talent and resources." Thom's assurance that Jack is impressed by me floats through my brain. "It's nice when people recognize your hard work and skills. It's even nicer when they lift you up instead of tearing you down."

"Yeah, well, I'm just here to get the kids. Emily wanted me to bring them home for a family dinner. She's learning to cook."

Home? Family?

I walk past him, not dignifying his comments with a response.

I do dignify them with an eye roll.

This is the first week that the mandated visits are in effect. He's not here because he wants to be but because he has to be. He must think his balls are made of steel. One swift kick would show him otherwise. Instead, I keep going, taking the high road. "I'll send them out."

And then I step inside and close the door, with him still standing there. Smiling, I open it back up. "Oh, and I'll drop the kids off to you on Friday night. You can bring them back on Sunday after two. And not before, as is explicitly written in the custody arrangement."

I close the door on his grumpy face, pumping my fist in victory.

Never during the course of our marriage would I have ordered him around like that. I would have been too afraid that he wouldn't like it. Screw him. I don't care what he likes anymore. I care about my kids, and they want to spend time with their father.

I hope he doesn't disappoint them. Let's face it, he's been nothing but a disappointment to me.

I quickly text Becky a recap of the incident with Mike. Before I know what I'm doing, I send a similar text to Thom. Things are ... different since last week when I went to his house. I was only there a brief time.

In fact, I sort of wandered out, my mind abuzz with too many things to properly say good-bye. It was only a few hours later that I even realized how awkward I must have seemed, drifting off and going home like that.

Luckily, Thom doesn't seem to get caught up on things like manners and social graces. I'd have been horribly offended if someone did something like that to me.

Mostly because I'd take it personally as a rejection, and it would drive me crazy wondering what I could have done differently or better to keep them from leaving.

I think I've spent more than half of my life trying to be different or better to keep someone from leaving.

Yet somehow I know that Thom and Becky will respond to my texts, even if I flake out every now and again. Aside from my kids, and they're not even full people yet, I think Becky—and now Thom—are the only people in the world who accept me as I am.

Not as I try to be.

I'm done trying to be perfect. It's an impossible task.

My body is literally genetically mutated and flawed, making perfection unattainable.

All this time, it's been futile to even try.

Texting is not enough for an epiphany this size.

I call Becky, and she declines my call. That means she's busy with something, not that she doesn't want to talk to me. I know this without a doubt.

Had it been Mike, I would have spent hours fretting over what I did to displease him and how to make it up to him.

Ugh.

I was such a loser.

No wonder he couldn't deal with me. It's a terrible burden to have to fill in the void left by others. I should know. I spent my entire childhood trying to do it for my mother.

The minute Thom answers, in lieu of a greeting or pleasantries, I say, "I'm not perfect, and I can't be."

"Thank you, Captain Obvious."

He's probably kidding, but his words still sting. I may have come to a realization, but it doesn't change over forty years of learned beliefs, no matter how erroneous.

"Mike didn't leave because I wasn't perfect. Or because I wasn't good enough."

"Mike left you because he's an ass. A dumbass, to be specific."

"Yes, but I may share some of the blame." I relate my thoughts about my constant need for validation and reassurance. "I'm sure that got old very quickly."

There's a bit of silence. It makes me uncomfortable.

"What?" I ask finally.

"Nothing. I'm just trying to picture you being insecure."

What?

"Maybe it's because you don't know me that well, but I'm probably the most insecure person you will ever meet."

"I doubt that. I've worked with musicians for the last twenty or thirty years. Those people are super messed up and super insecure. Notoriously so."

I consider that.

Thom continues, "Your competence and overall togetherness is something that is admired, feared, and strikes envy in all those who see."

I laugh. "I doubt that. What are you doing right now?"

"Aren't you supposed to ask me what I'm wearing?"

"I know the answer to that question. A Hawaiian shirt." I roll my eyes at the thought of it.

"Wrong. I'm wearing a T-shirt I got from a Jimmy Buffet concert I went to in 1998."

"You, not in your trademark shirt? This I gotta see!"

"Come on over. I don't leave the house like this."

"I should pass tonight. I've got things to do."

As much as I'm tempted, I have to do homework checks and make sure everyone is doing what they should. Since the night I lost my shit on them, the kids have been doing better.

But then I remember that the kids went with Mike for their "family" time. I'm here by myself. I can go if I want to.

I don't think it ever occurred to them that I might not be okay. Or perhaps it's because I didn't let them see it. I only wanted them to see my perfection and not my flaws.

Of course, if I make the decision to go flat, there will never be any perception of perfection again.

I believe I can live with that.

CHAPTER 30

"Hey."

All the words I practiced on the way over, my explanations and excuses for dropping in after declining his offer to come over, fly out of my head.

"Hey yourself." Thom steps aside, swinging the door open. "I had my spiel all prepared for the Jehovah's or Mormons or cable TV people. I'm a little disappointed I won't get to use it."

"Sorry to disappoint you." I step inside.

"You are never a disappointment, Margot. Quite the contrary."

His use of my name reminds me. "What's with the Lady K stuff on the radio?" We're standing awkwardly in his foyer. He motions toward his living room, so I walk in and sit down on his couch. It seriously looks like something out of a 50s or 60s movie set. I would never in a million years pick out a single thing in this room, yet somehow, it suits Thom to a T.

Quirky yet comfortable.

"I didn't figure you wanted your real name out there. And if you never thought about it, you don't want your real name out there. There are some wackos listening, so you don't want to be too easy to find. There aren't too many Margots floating around and even fewer Margs."

"But Lady K?"

"Isn't your last name Kensington? I thought you sounded like someone in the British royal family. When you are not going apeshit on me, you carry yourself like that too."

Once again, I'm at a loss for words.

"Do you want a drink?" Thom asks. I shake my head, though I should probably say yes to be polite. Then it occurs to me that it won't matter to Thom if I'm polite or not.

"No thank you."

I can't abandon all my habits.

"I ... I'm not sure why I'm here."

"That makes two of us, but I'm glad you stopped by. You've got a lot on your plate right now."

"I don't want to talk about me anymore. I feel like that's all we do."

"It is." Thom smiles.

"Tell me about you. I mean, I've learned a little from listening to you on the radio. You don't seem to hold much back, do you?"

He shrugs, settling down on the armchair across from me. He stretches out, putting his bare feet up on the ottoman. His T-shirt, even with a parrot on it, seems tame compared to his typical bright shirts. If I saw him on the street, I don't know that I'd recognize him. Tonight, all I can see is that his eyes are just a shade or two lighter than the brown of his hair and that his five o'clock shadow is just the right amount of stubble.

All I ever see is the shirt.

"You always wear the shirts so that when you want to blend in, people don't recognize you, don't you?"

He smiles tightly. "Over the past few years, I've come to value my privacy a little more. But it's a hard balancing act, given my profession. It's not like I'm cut out to wear a suit and sit at a desk."

"Plus, you're good at what you do."

"There's that. But I've been at it a while, and there are some drawbacks."

"Like what?" I can't imagine. He has a nice house, a fancy car, and comes and goes as he pleases, without a care for what other people think of him. He doesn't have to worry that he can't make his mortgage payment.

It must be nice.

And regardless of that, people like him. He doesn't even have to try.

Hell, I hated him, just on principle, and yet here I find myself, eager to hear his life story.

"Come on, Marg. Think about it. I'm going to die alone."

It hits me. He's going through some of the same things that I am. I mean, *obviously* because of UnBRCAble, but I never thought about it before now.

"I'm a terrible friend. At least to you. Usually I'm not, but you caught me at a bad ... year."

"I think you've had a lot of bad years."

I consider this. "I don't know that I ever would have thought that. I thought my life was perfect."

"Didn't anyone ever tell you, there's no such thing?"

I laugh. "I think I'm learning that. So tell me about your imperfect life."

"I'm a bastard. I'm selfish. I'm lazy. It depends on which of my wives you ask."

"How many wives are there?"

"None currently, two in the past and an almost wife."

"What happened?" I'm trying to picture Thom as the happy husband, but I can't. He seems like the perpetual bachelor.

"One wanted me to be something I wasn't. One wanted me for what I could do for her, rather than for me. And the almost wife was just straight-up poor decision-making."

I have to laugh. "You could probably say anyone who becomes an ex is poor decision-making." I think about what he said. "What did she want you to be?"

"She wanted me to be a doting husband and father. To be here in the morning and available in the evening. When you land the morning slot, you throw those things out the window. I don't go to evening things. UnBRCAble is about as late as I'm ever out. It's not super compatible with someone who's a night owl."

"Yeah, I bet you never saw each other." I try to picture Mike working those hours. It would have been awful, especially when the kids were little.

"She—Miranda—knew it coming in. But she wanted me to change and give up everything, including my career, to fit her vision."

Exactly as I did with Mike.

"I wasn't there fifteen years ago. Maybe now, but I resented being asked to change. I am who I am. Accept me or leave me. So she did."

Oh to have that confidence.

Thom gets up and goes into the kitchen. A minute later he comes back with two glasses of white wine. "I have a feeling this conversation is going to require liquid lubricant."

"Is that the official divorce-discussion rule? I'm new to this."

"There's a handbook you should familiarize yourself with, including receiving advice from everybody and their brother."

"Yes. Mike hadn't even been gone three days when my mother told me I needed to be dating again. As if that's ever going to happen."

"Ever?"

I wave at my chest. "Yeah, um, I don't think so. I mean, what I have going on is not compatible with dating, and when I go flat, I don't know how I'd ever bring that up. No one's going to want to date a middle-aged, divorced woman with no boobs."

Thom takes a long sip of his wine, looking at me over the rim of his glass. "You don't know that."

My mouth is suddenly dry.

And if I'm not mistaken, my heart rate speeds up a bit.

258

I clear my throat. "And what about ex-Mrs. Jones number two?"

"She was in it for the fame. She wanted me for who I could introduce her to."

"Oh, did she leave you for a rock star or something?"

"No, I just got sick and tired of her using me. I don't think she really loved me at all. She only loved what she thought she could get from me."

"I'm so sorry," I say quietly.

"I mean, I should have known that someone who looked like she did wouldn't really be interested in someone like me."

I cock my head, taking him in. Straight nose. Good teeth. Wry smile. "Why would you say that?"

He waves his hand in front of his face. "Is your vision okay?"

"My vision is stellar. You know I have an issue with your shirts, but other than that, the look works for you. Quite pleasant. Not a face that belongs in radio."

He smiles, his eyes crinkling with warmth and sparkle. "Thank you for saying that, Margot, even though you must be drunk."

I look at my glass, with barely three sips out of it. "Yes, I'm hammered. Totally plastered. That's the only logical explanation."

In the moments of silence following, I wonder what he's thinking about. I wonder if he knows what I'm thinking about. That in another world—another life— maybe we could be good together. Obviously not in my reality though.

But we could be friends, which I don't think I would have been able to say four months ago.

"You know, you've gone through a lot this year," Thom says finally.

"I'm aware."

"I think you should talk about it. On the air. I think women would like to hear what you have to say. You could be a voice for women's health and life after divorce and resilience and all that kind of crap. And it might help you work through things. It has for me."

"So eloquent. But that'd be a no. Are you crazy? I can't get on the air and talk about that sort of stuff. I'm not even cut out to be on the air. I feel like a bumbling idiot whenever the mic is on ... and even when it's not. Need I remind you about the rogue breast prosthetic incident?"

Thom puts his hand up to his mouth, pretending he's coughing.

I sit up a little straighter. "Are you laughing at me?" I put my wine glass down. "It's not funny."

Thom tilts his head. "It was kind of funny. But only because I was trying to help you, and you put up such a fuss. That was the funny part. Well, that and the falling over. You have to admit, you've been some really good material for the show."

Now I'm on my feet. "My life falling apart is not entertainment. All my life, all I've ever wanted was to get things right."

"Let me guess ... perfect?" Thom says the word like it leaves a bad taste in his mouth. He rises as well, stepping close to me.

"Is that so wrong? Yet all you do is mock my failures for the world to see. Er, hear. Whatever. But they're *my* failures. They're not entertainment." I turn to leave. "Thank you for the drink and the conversation. It was nice of you to invite me in."

As I'm walking out the door, I hear Thom say, "See you tomorrow at work, Margot."

Ugh.

I'm never escaping him, am I?

First thing, I'm going in to Jack and telling him I'm not going on air anymore. What I'm going through is too personal to share.

CHAPTER 31

"So, we need to talk."

Usually, it's not a good sign when someone starts the conversation this way, but considering everything I've assumed Jack Smalls ever thought was wrong, I'm going to keep an open mind.

Well, I'll *try* to keep an open mind. This is me we're talking about here.

Also, since I need to talk to Jack too, this might be a good start.

"As you know, Todd is having some health problems. He needs to take some extended time off to take care of himself. We'd like you to fill in for him. It would change your hours and your responsibilities here."

"Yeah, Jack, about that, I don't think I want to do that."

"But you and TJ are so good together. You have a chemistry that you just can't predict or plan for. You're a natural. Seriously, is there anything you can't do?"

"Nurse a baby." The answer flies out of my mouth before I can help it. "Sorry. Mastectomy humor."

Jack's face turns red.

"Sorry. I figured since the—incident—on the news, you knew. I don't have breasts anymore. Sorry." Jesus, why can't I stop talking? "Anyway—"

"Right, I know you have family responsibilities. Could you get here for seven? Or even seven-thirty? I mean, the earlier the better, obviously, but we're willing to work with you. The earlier hours will of course mean you get done earlier, if that's any incentive."

My mind is already whirling with ways to get out the door and guarantee that both of my kids still arrive at school. "I'll ... have to ..."

"Obviously, it'll change your responsibilities around here, though would you be willing to show the new hire your system?"

"New hire?"

"Yes, you'll be considered talent, so no more swag room for you, though I can't thank you enough for what you've done with that. I had no idea that things could run this well."

"I'll be the talent?"

I can't seem to stop asking dumb questions.

"Yes, so as such, your salary will increase. It's not that much of an increase, but you don't technically have any experience in the field." I glance at the paper he's handing to me. It's almost ten dollars more per hour than I'm currently making, plus I know there're extra bonuses for those appearances I'm used to attending anyway.

It certainly would ease my mind a little with the mortgage. Then I probably would be able to stay in the house and not uproot the kids. Jordan only has one more year of high school left. The last thing I want to do is traumatize them further by making them leave the only house they've ever known.

I want to say yes, but then I remember Thom wanting me to use it as a platform to talk about my boob and divorce stuff.

Ugh, no.

I do not want to put myself out there like that, and Thom would push me to. Without a doubt.

I'm about to say no when I see the poster, peeking out from behind Jack's desk.

"TJ the DJ and Lady K in the morning."

There's a professional headshot of Thom, complete with trademark shirt and lollipop. And a picture of me, wearing my WBRC shirt, yelling into the microphone during the Red Cross event at the mall.

You know, the one where my fake boob fell out.

I squint at the picture, trying to see if you can tell that my prosthetic is about to jump ship and mortify me until the end of time.

"You had ... posters printed up?"

"TJ ran it off for me."

"TJ."

"Yeah, it was his idea. He knew you'd do it. Said you wouldn't let him down."

"Said I ... wouldn't let him ... down?" I ask, struggling to make sense of this all.

"Yeah. He pointed out how dependable you were and how you cared about what people thought of WBRC. That you wanted us to look good."

Un huh.

That's all I want to hear from Jack Smalls.

The only person who owes me an explanation is Thom.

I stand up without saying anything and snatch a poster. "I'm taking this." Leaving abruptly, I march down the hall to Thom's office where he's working on material for the show tomorrow.

The show that I'm sure he thought I'd be co-hosting with him.

"What's this?" I slam the poster down on his desk. He glances up, cocking an eyebrow.

"It was a mock-up. You'll need to get a more professional picture."

Obviously.

"Did you send this one out?"

He nods. "To Jack. He must have liked it. It's funny."

"Why? How could you do this to me? Why would you do this to me? I didn't say yes."

"Think about it, Margot. You have fun doing it, and it might be good for you."

"What? Why?"

Thom sits back in his chair, folding his arms across his chest. "It's helpful to get things out."

"Things? What things?" My voice is loud, but I don't care.

"You know, your divorce. Your ex. Your kids. Your breast cancer and BRCA journey."

"You want me to get on the airwaves and talk about all the ways in which I've failed in life? Have you lost your ever-lovin' mind?" Now I'm full-on mom yelling.

"You talk about things in UnBRCAble, and that helps, doesn't it?"

I slam my fists on his desk, leaning in and hissing, "There's a difference between talking about things in a support group with a close group of people going through similar experiences and getting on the air and hanging out my dirty laundry to dry. I can't believe ... I thought you understood me. You don't understand me at all."

"I do though. Don't you see that?"

"Thom, you don't know me in the least." Even as I say it, I know it's not true. However, the train has left the station, and I'm clinging onto the railing for dear life. "If you knew me, you'd know I don't want to be out there, exposing all my weaknesses. It's like you want to show the world what a failure I am. Do you get off on it? Does it make you feel better about your own terrible, lonely life? Is that how you build yourself up—by pushing someone else down? You're just like those bullies who tormented me throughout all of school. Are you happy that you found someone in even worse shape than you?"

"Worse shape? Bully? How do you see that?" There's an edge to Thom's voice I've never heard before.

"Living alone. Craving the spotlight but not knowing how actually to deal with it. You're lost. Adrift. And now you want to bring me down with you."

"What I want is for you to stop assuming the worst about me every single time. Now I know why you're so thin. You get all of that exercise constantly jumping to conclusions."

Asshole.

I turn and storm out.

But I don't know where to go. My desk is in the middle of the room, and everyone's looking at me. Great. I might as well Facebook Live this meltdown too, because just as many people witnessed this one.

I walk down the hall to the back room. No one ever comes in here, and maybe I can stay in here forever.

My phone pings with a text notification.

It's Bailey.

Emily is a big Red Hot Chili Peppers fan. Can you get me tickets to give to her?

I stare at the phone for a beat, wondering what I ever did to the universe to deserve this. Why would my daughter ask this of me?

Why? I text back.

Because I want her to like me.

Oh, my poor daughter, falling into my footsteps.

I don't know what I can do—seeing as how I'm probably quitting. Afraid to let her down, I quickly add:

I can probably get a picture or something. Will that be ok?

She doesn't answer right away. Great. She's probably mad at me for not coming through for her. I don't know Emily and don't know how she feels about either one of my children. I should probably find out. I add it to my mental to-do list.

My phone buzzes, indicating an email. It's from Jack, reiterating the job offer, including the salary.

It's almost double what I'm making now.

How can I say no to that?

Principles. That's how.

I will not allow myself to be bullied into doing something I'm not comfortable with. I don't need to talk about my dead marriage to get over it. I don't need to speak about my louse of an ex-husband or that it's killing me that my daughter wants to impress his girlfriend.

Becky and I will dissect this for days, if not weeks on end, and then I'll feel better.

But that's different. That's talking to a friend. Not thousands of strangers.

My phone buzzes again. It's another email from Jack.

These have been coming in for you, but since you didn't have a public station email, either TJ or I have been receiving them. Happy reading!

Then, my phone starts buzzing like someone playing the game Operation after drinking six shots of espresso.

Thank you for talking about breast cancer the other day. Sometimes I feel like I'm the only one who knows what it's like.

After hearing that you were diagnosed so young, I scheduled my mammogram. Thank you!

My mom died from breast cancer and my oldest sister was diagnosed. I'm scared she's going to die too. What should I do?

With the last one, my immediate thought is that the writer should be tested for BRCA or some other genetic cause of cancer.

Thank you for talking about wearing prosthetics. I feel so much shame every time I put them in. I'm always afraid what happened to you will happen to me. But you survived it. Maybe I can too!

I want to hug each one of these women. Half of them need to join UnBRCAble. I need to email them all back. Oh God, that's going to take forever.

Or … I could just talk about it on the radio.

CHAPTER 32

"I'm not ready for this. I don't want to do this. I don't need to do this."

Thom adjusts his headset. "Yes, you are, and yes, you do. It helps you."

"No, it does ... okay fine, it does, but I still don't want to do this." I cross my arms over my chest like a petulant child.

"Don't want to do it or don't want to *need* to do it?"

In lieu of a reply, I stick my tongue out at Thom.

"At some point, you will have to learn how to push the buttons and not just sit there being a pretty face, you know," Thom whispers before pushing some button. A light flashes indicating that we're live.

"Welcome back. In studio today, I've got with me Lady K. Todd is taking some time off to work on his health. We'll miss you, buddy, but take care of you. And, Krista, I'm sorry that he's home all the time now. But for those of us listening, Lady K will be sharing the morning commute with us."

I pull out my list of topics to talk about. Just because I'm doing a job in which I'm no way qualified doesn't mean I show up unprepared. Also, if I have a list, I'm less likely to go off on Thom, which I feel like doing.

This is so far out of my comfort zone, it's not even on the map.

"Whatcha got there, Lady K?" Thom squints across the studio at me.

"I … um …" Crap. I can't say um. Why am I so nervous? Oh right, because I'm thinking about it. When I've been on the air before, Thom threw me in, so I didn't have time to freak out and overanalyze. I take a deep breath and start again. "I came up with a list of topics to talk about. You know me, I like to be prepared."

"And you know me, I like to upset the apple cart."

"Especially my apple cart."

Thom smiles. "Especially yours. So, for the good people listening out there, tell us a little about yourself."

"You can't be serious. I hate those open-ended questions. I never know what to say or how much to say or what someone wants to hear. Gah. Okay, I'm a newly divorced mom of two teenagers. I'm a breast cancer survivor. I'd describe myself as reliable and diligent, and I basically have no idea what I'm doing here."

"Tell me one thing that your kids hate when you do."

I wrinkle my brow at Thom. Why this question? It seems odd. "I love Facebook memes, so I send them to my kids all the time. They think they're stupid. I can't help it if they don't have a sense of humor. They inherited that from their father."

"So how are things going with the divorce?"

As much as I want to launch into a tirade about what an ass my ex-husband is, he's still my children's father, so it would only hurt them. "You know, I was totally blindsided by it. I didn't see it coming at all. But I do have to say, perhaps I've been finding myself a bit more since he left. I stopped worrying about pleasing him and have focused on pleasing myself."

Thom arches an eyebrow.

Oh God, what have I said?

"Not *pleasing* pleasing myself but making myself happy. Giving me my own happy ending instead of relying on him to do it."

"Lady K, you're not making this any better."

I wad up my list and throw it at Thom.

"But I get what you're saying." He laughs. "I only knew you a little bit while you were still married, but from what I know, the focus was on making him happy. Now, you are making sure that you are. Is that what you were trying to say?"

I nod and then realize the listeners can't hear my head rattle. "Yes, exactly. And I need to focus on myself right now, as I've had some health struggles this year."

"Okay, put a pin in that thought and we'll get back to it after we play some music."

Thom clicks a few buttons, and our indicator light goes out. "See, that wasn't so bad."

"Except for when I accidentally started talking about masturbation, it was fine. Perfect start, really."

"There you are using that *p* word again. You really need to knock it out of your vocabulary. Okay, in the next segment, we're going to talk BRCA stuff. You ready?"

No.

"Sure. I guess I have to rip the Band-Aid off at some point, right? After all, it's why I'm here."

"You're here because you have a gift for this, and we work well together."

"Not to mention peer pressure and I have to pay the bills."

Thom winks at me. "Well, there's that." He clicks the buttons again.

"Okay so, Lady K, you and I know each other outside of work. Want to talk about that?"

"Yes, well, fun fact about me. You and Todd actually gave me the Jerk-Face Award just before Christmas. I still think I *don't* deserve it, but I'm willing to contend that perhaps in that moment I was not my best self."

"That's an understatement." Thom's clicking away on his computer. "Here, give me a second to pull the clip up. Lady K, do you want to set the scene?"

"Both TJ and I carry the genetic mutation on the BRCA genes. This is most commonly called the 'breast cancer' gene. I had my first lump removed when I was thirty-six and had a mastectomy when I was thirty-eight. It's a tough club to have membership to, but I found a great group of ladies for support. So every week, I went to this group, and we talked about lots of personal things, because this cancer affects our women bits. And then one day, there's TJ the DJ, sitting in my lady group. I did not take it well."

"Oh no, you did not."

"It's hard to talk about the status of your nipples in front of a strange man."

"Yet you just mentioned it to thousands of listeners."

"Yes, but the listeners can't see my face turn beet red, and their eyes don't immediately drop to my chest when I start talking about it."

"For the record, I am not looking at Lady K's chest, though I am trying to get a peek at Smudge the Producer's through the glass."

I have to give it to him—Thom has excellent timing.

Thom cues up the clip. After, he nods in my direction. "Do you have a rebuttal?"

"I was rude to you, I admit it. However, it still took some getting used to. There are definitely lady things that are more easily talked about without a male there. No doubt."

"Agreed. And there are things I don't want to hear about either. Some lady things are best kept mysterious."

"I will concede that my verbal response *probably* deserved a Jerk-Face Award, but my intent did not. Thankfully, you and I have come to a truce—of sorts—and we have moved on, regardless of award status."

"I still like to push your buttons. It's fun to see you get all frazzled."

"I'm glad my distress results in your pleasure. I'm here to serve."

"No, what I like is you get all frazzled, which you *hate* to be, and then you rise up, stronger and straighter than before. It's amazing, really. But being amazing is your superpower."

I feel a tear start to threaten the corner of my eye. "I'm going to need to remember that coming up. I've got a big road still ahead of me."

"Even if all the roads that lead you there are winding?"

"And even if all the lights that lead me there are blinding."

I've never understood the lyrics to Oasis's "Wonderwall" until this moment. As if he's reading my mind, Thom starts the song.

"You're going to be the one who saves me," I say to him frankly.

"No, you're going to save yourself. I'm just showing you the way to do it."

"I'm sorry I didn't want you in my nipple group."

"I'm sorry we have to be in the nipple group."

I know what he's saying. Sorry we have this inherent biological curse that may end both our lives.

"I'm not sorry we're in the group though."

"Me neither."

EPILOGUE

"Are you ready? This is big."

I nod. I'm not ready. I don't know that I ever will be, but if I've learned one thing about myself this year, it's that sometimes I need a gentle push—or shove—to start me into motion.

I love my new blazer. A shade of peacock blue that makes my eyes stand out. Slim black pants. Ballet flats because, well, Thom and I stand almost eye to eye as it is.

No shirt.

Just the blazer.

I know exactly how I want to pose. I've been practicing it in the mirror all week. Bailey has been helping me. If anyone knows how to pose for a camera, it's a fourteen-year-old girl with social media access.

Both Jordan and Bailey wanted to come to this. They both said they wanted to support me. While I believe that's true, I also think they were hoping to get pulled from school for this.

So it's Thom and I and the photographer. My hair is blown out, and my makeup is flawless. I add a pendant necklace. It's got two charms on it: a lotus flower to symbolize overcoming struggles and a musical flat symbol.

Becky gave it to me as a present following my surgery, and I wear it every day.

"Let's do this," the photographer calls.

I step into the center of the backdrop and tell Thom, "This is how I'm posing. You can figure out how to work around me."

"Whatever you wish, Lady K."

I stand up tall, hands on my hips, shoulders squared. It opens up the blazer enough to see the medial edges of my scars, and that I have no contouring to my bust line, but it's still "decent."

Thom stands behind me and leans his chin on my shoulder. After a few clicks, he shifts, imitating my posture, just off to the side. Then, Thom moves, threading his arms around my waist. I turn my head to look at him. He smiles and says, "Are you ticklish?"

I burst out laughing in anticipation, forgetting that we're being photographed.

"That's great, guys. I totally got it."

"Already?"

"Yup." The photographer starts packing up his things. "You two are naturals. You are great together. You seem more like a couple than co-workers."

Thom slides his arms out from around my waist. He takes my hand, tucking my whole arm into his side as if we were in some Victorian setting rather than a downtown photo studio. Then he leans down and kisses my knuckles. "Where to? It seems a shame to waste such a perfectly good hair and makeup day."

"Hang on, I need to put a shirt on. It's one thing to appear on a magazine cover like this, but it's another thing to walk into Applebee's."

"Applebee's? Really."

"No, but you know what I mean. Mainstream America isn't ready—"

"For a gorgeous, empowered woman who takes no shit."

"And doesn't have breasts."

"I always told you, I'm more of an ass man."

I head into the ladies' room to quickly pull a fitted white T-shirt on. I wear a lot of fitted tops now, and it doesn't bother me that I don't have the silhouette I used to. I mean, sure, I miss my cleavage, but being flat has so many advantages.

First off, no more surgeries. As promised, Dr. Chung gave me a smooth finish, and now I can stay off his table forever.

Second, no more implant illness. I never realized how sick I was until they were taken out.

Third, I have my best shot at living a long healthy life.

Fourth, I have an entire drawer back in my dresser. Also, bras are really uncomfortable. And, I never have to worry about embarrassing nipples showing when I'm cold.

The thing that I didn't see coming was the sense of empowerment. I took my health into my own hands—Dr. Chung's actually—and it is a rush. I feel like Wonder Woman all the time.

Well, a lot of the time.

And that makes me feel sexy.

Like a woman.

Who would have thought my absent chest would make me feel more feminine? It's certainly better than having the foobs that always felt so alien. That made me aware every single day of my imperfections and flaws. That made me feel like I was covering up and hiding a dark secret.

Now the secret is out for the world to see—and hear. It's not that I don't want people to like me, because I still do. But now, as I'm growing to love myself, the approval of others matters less.

Thom walks out of the bathroom and my heart skips a beat. When we go out in public, he hangs up the Hawaiian shirt.

Thank goodness.

Today, he's wearing charcoal gray trousers and a matching vest with an eggplant dress shirt, rolled at the forearms. If I had to guess, I'd say he's wearing suspenders too.

Much like his house, he looks as if he's stepped out of a Rat Pack movie, with as much charm and swag as Frank Sinatra and Dean Martin. He's even slicked his hair down to the side a bit.

I wish he could have been photographed like this.

"I feel underdressed."

"No, you look great. Beautiful. You ready to go?"

I nod.

On this late fall afternoon, the crispness in the air hints at winter. I slide into the Oldsmobile and point the heating vent toward me. Then my phone buzzes with an email notification.

"It's the article. Are you ready?" I ask Thom nervously.

"Shouldn't I be asking you that question?"

I click it open and immediately smile at the title.

Flat-Out Fantastic.

It's not every day you get a feature in *People Magazine*.

Morning Meltdown with TJ the DJ featuring Lady K has been a media sensation. Mostly because of our candid openness about living with BRCA gene mutations. The audience has followed my surgical journey. You should have seen the number of flowers and candy and gifts I received at the station.

We took them all into local nursing homes. Well, except for a dozen Cider Belly Doughnuts that I received because, well, who could resist?

My kids are impressed with my celebrity status. I mean, as much as they can be considering they're still teenagers and radio is "so 1990s," according to Bailey. Yet still, there was some ooh-ing and aaah-ing when the pictures of me with Anthony Kiedis and Flea from the Red Hot Chili Peppers happened to find their way to my Instagram account.

No, I didn't get Emily tickets or even an autograph. That picture was for her.

And somewhere along the way, it occurred to my kids that I can't work and do it all and that they indeed have time to vacuum or do the dishes. By being less available to them, they're becoming the self-sufficient humans I'd always hoped they'd become.

Turns out, if you do everything for them, they only learn that you can do everything better than them. Definitely not a perfect parenting moment there.

Also, I try not to laugh when the kids tell me about how their father is freaking out all the time because Emily isn't much of a housekeeper, nor does she act as his personal assistant, and he can't function like that.

I do think I'm nailing the divorce thing though. It turns out that old saying was right. Living well is the best revenge. I'd originally had ideas about hanging Mike out to dry on the radio, exposing him for the louse he is, but as I got more settled into investing in myself, the less revenge mattered.

The less he mattered.

Most of my life is not perfect. I'm busy and that lack of privacy thing can get old. Thom and I are ... figuring it out.

A typical romance was not in the cards for me this year, but Thom and I are anything but typical.

We had an emotional connection long before I saw it going anywhere else. I'm not sure how the next part will go. I still have a lifetime of baggage to deal with, and Thom's dealing with his own stuff. Yet somehow, I know things are heading in the right direction. If I had to predict, I'd say this next chapter of my life is going to be perfect.

Imperfectly perfect.

THE END

ACKNOWLEDGMENTS

Writing a book in the midst of a pandemic was certainly a challenging experience. Once again thank you to Erin Huss for the inspiration and guidance for the entire UnBRCAble Women Series.

Thank you to Sarah Cantara for answering my questions about working in radio. I hope my creative liberties weren't too creative.

For the Friday night Zoom crew who helped me keep what few wits I have left: Becky, Melissa, Erin, Laura, Wendy, and Whitney. Laughter really is the best medicine.

Tami Lund, thank you for stepping up and stepping in with your editing skills. I really hope you didn't have to stick a fork in your eye.

Thank you to Chrissy Wolfe for the proofreading. I had no idea I made that many mistakes.

To the women of BRCAStrong who welcomed me into their bubble. These books are for you.

Thanks to the hubs for coming up with the idea to finally finish converting the playroom into a real, grown up office. I can't say it helps with my productivity, but I love this space.

Jake and Sophia, the kids in this book are no way based on you. Not even a little. Okay, a little. Actually maybe more than a little. Someday we will look back on the teen years and laugh. I hope.

To Mom and Dad: You definitely come in first place as my own personal cheerleaders.

ABOUT THE AUTHOR

Telling stories of resilient women, *USA Today* Bestselling Author Kathryn R. Biel hails from Upstate New York where her most important role is being mom and wife to an incredibly understanding family who don't mind fetching coffee and living in a dusty house. In addition to being Chief Home Officer and Director of Child Development of the Biel household, she works as a school-based physical therapist. She attended Boston University and received her Doctorate in Physical Therapy from The Sage Colleges. After years of writing countless letters of medical necessity for wheelchairs, finding increasingly creative ways to encourage insurance companies to fund her client's needs, and writing entertaining annual Christmas letters, she decided to take a shot at writing the kind of novel that she likes to read. Kathryn is the author of many women's fiction, romantic comedy, contemporary romance, and chick lit works, including the award-winning books, *Live for This, Made for Me*, and *Underneath It All*.

Scan now to instantly receive FREE exclusive bonus content!

Stand Alone Books:
Good Intentions
Hold Her Down
I'm Still Here
Jump, Jive, and Wail
Killing Me Softly
Live for This
Once in a Lifetime
Paradise by the Dashboard Light

A New Beginnings Series:
Completions and Connections: A New Beginnings Novella
Made for Me
New Attitude
Queen of Hearts

The UnBRCAble Women Series:
Ready for Whatever
Seize the Day
Underneath It All

Center State Love Story Series:
Take a Chance on Me
Vision of Love
Whatever It Takes

Boston Buzzards:
XOXO
You Belong with Me

If you've enjoyed this book, please help the author out by leaving a review on your favorite vendor website and **Goodreads**. A few minutes of your time makes a huge difference to an indie author!

Made in the USA
Coppell, TX
09 May 2023

16595104R00166